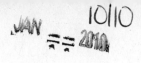

TEN LESSONS FOR KASPAR SNIT

Cary Fagan

Tundra Books

Published in Canada by Tundra Books,
75 Sherbourne Street, Toronto, Ontario M5A 2P9

Published in the United States by Tundra Books of Northern New York,
P.O. Box 1030, Plattsburgh, New York 12901

Library of Congress Control Number: 2007938542

Library and Archives Canada Cataloguing in Publication

Fagan, Cary
   Ten lessons for Kaspar Snit / Cary Fagan.

Sequel to: The fortress of Kaspar Snit and Directed by Kaspar Snit.
ISBN 978-0-88776-835-4

   I. Title.

PS8561.A375T44 2008   JC813'.54   C2007-906099-4

We acknowledge the financial support of the Government of Canada
through the Book Publishing Industry Development Program (BPIDP)
and that of the Government of Ontario through the Ontario Media
Development Corporation's Ontario Book Initiative. We further
acknowledge the support of the Canada Council for the Arts and the
Ontario Arts Council for our publishing program.

ONTARIO ARTS COUNCIL
CONSEIL DES ARTS DE L'ONTARIO

Design: Terri Nimmo
Typeset in Plantin

Printed and bound in Canada

1 2 3 4 5 6   13 12 11 10 09 08

For Rachel,
number one (or is it two?) daughter

THE
CREATURE
CATCHER

"Oh, no. This is terrible," groaned my father, folding back a page of the morning newspaper. "Just listen to this."

We were all having breakfast – Dad, Mom, me, and my younger brother, Solly – and all of us, except my dad, were rushing. Solly and I had to get to school, Mom had to get to her job at the passport office, but Dad didn't have to rush anywhere, not even to his office in the garage. He was the world's foremost expert on fountains but, at the moment, the fountain business was slow and he was still wearing his pajamas, bathrobe, and slippers.

"What is it, Manfred?" said Mom, brushing her hair, even as she chomped on a piece of toast.

"Eleanor, you listen especially," said Dad. He sounded serious. Peering through his new reading glasses, he cleared his throat and began.

CREATURE CATCHER STALKS
MYSTERIOUS FLYING GIRL
Special to the Sentinel

Standing outside city hall yesterday, famous "Creature Catcher" Levon du Plessy-Minsk announced that he has begun a search for our own local myth, the Mysterious Flying Girl.

As almost everyone knows, the Mysterious Flying Girl was first seen on national television last year, when she helped to defeat Kaspar Snit. That infamous evil genius, masquerading as a television director and aided by his assistant, Marvin Slouchovsky – otherwise known as Slouch – had been trying to steal the one million dollars meant to help the people of Verulia after the earthquake.

This newspaper posted a reward of one thousand dollars for proof that the Mysterious Flying Girl is not a fake. Many have attempted to prove her existence, but so far all have failed. Last week the Sentinel *upped the reward by ten dollars.*

"It takes an expert to catch one of these rare creatures," Levon du Plessy-Minsk told the press. He was dressed like an explorer, in a pith helmet, hunter's vest, and camouflage trousers. "They are smart, quick, and sometimes

dangerous. Trust me, I know. I've stalked the hairy Bigfoot in the northern reaches of Canada. I've dived into a lake in Scotland to swim with the Loch Ness Monster. If anyone can catch this flying girl, it's me."

Levon du Plessy-Minsk showed off his minivan, specially equipped with radar detector, cameras, and other spying devices. *"I'll catch her,"* he said. *"And I'll collect that one thousand and ten dollars. And when I've got her, I'll put her on display for the whole world to see."*

Will the Creature Catcher really catch the Mysterious Flying Girl? Keep reading the Sentinel *to find out.*

"The nerve of that man!" fumed my mother, swallowing the last of her coffee. "Display my daughter? What does he think she is – some sort of . . . of . . ."

"Freak?" Solly suggested.

"I don't want to hear that word in this house."

"How about weirdo? Misfit? Mutant?"

"That's enough, Solly."

I was glad Mom said it. Otherwise, I was going to have to dump the remains of my cereal on Solly's head.

"It isn't just Eleanor who's at risk," Dad said. "Anybody in this family who flies could get caught. We're going to have to make sure that Levon du Plessy-Minsk gets discouraged and goes away."

"Don't tell me," I said. "That means –"

"That's right, Eleanor. No flying until further notice."

"How about gliding?" said Solly.

3

"No."

"How about taking off really fast, doing a loop, and then crashing down into a swimming pool?"

"I said no, Solly."

Feeling miserable, I swished the remaining cereal around in my bowl. "I hate Levon du Plessy-Minsk."

"Are you sure you don't have a crush on him?" Solly said. "Because that's what you and Julia Worthington like to talk about these days. Boys."

"Have you been spying again?"

"Anyway, I know it isn't that old Creature Catcher you like," Solly said. "It's that new boy in school – the one with the funny name. What is it? River? Porcupine? Tulip?"

"His name is Fox. And I never said I liked him."

"You have a boy in your class named Fox?" asked Dad.

"Maybe you can give him your photograph," said Solly. *"To cutesy-putesy Foxy-Woxy from your Elly-Smelly. Kiss, kiss, kiss, kiss. . . ."*

"ELEANOR!" Mom and Dad screamed together, but it was too late. I'd already dumped my cereal bowl over Solly's head. Soggy flakes dripped down his forehead.

Solly stuck out his tongue and caught a flake sliding down his face. "Pretty sweet," he said.

THE
LOMOX
COMMITTEE

I had to wait for Solly to get cleaned up before we could walk to school. He had become so annoying that, the other day, I announced to my parents that I was going to move out. Then they reminded me that I was thirteen. But I have this to say about Solly: he doesn't hold a grudge. As soon as we were outside, he forgot all about my pouring cereal over his head.

On the sidewalk, we stopped for a moment to look at our fountain. It took up the entire front yard, with its eight larger-than-life winged horses rearing up on their hind legs, each horse with a buck-naked rider holding a conch shell. I used to be embarrassed by the statue when I was younger, but now I had gotten used to it, and even our neighbors had decided they liked it. The only thing was, lately I had become embarrassed all over again. Not because of the naked figures, but because of the green algae growing in the enormous basin underneath, the streaks of pigeon poop on the riders' heads, and the dirty plastic bag caught on the ear of one of the horses. My dad had always held a fountain-cleaning day every three months, that is, until he stopped getting any work and started spending the day in his bathrobe. Now the fountain was a neglected eyesore. Every time we saw Mr. Worthington next door, he muttered about falling real-estate values.

We started walking to school. As always, Solly wore his full Googoo-man outfit: green pajamas (the top damp from milk) with a red bathing suit pulled over them, rubber bathing cap, goggles (a new pair because the old ones had gotten cracked), belt, and shoes with retractable roller skates. Because he had grown, the pajamas were too small and you could see his ankles and wrists. Also, he had a new cape. The old towel had become so tattered that he'd had to replace it. This towel had on it the words BIG BURP COLA HAS TEN BURPS IN EVERY BOTTLE.

"Eleanor?" Solly said, looking up at the sky.

"Uh-huh?"

"Do you think if a person stood in the sun long enough, he would melt?"

"Where do you get these ideas?"

"I wonder about that myself sometimes."

We were just across the street from Ginger Hirshbein's old house. Ginger had been Solly's best friend, but he and his family had moved to Cow Head, Newfoundland. The house had remained empty for a long time, but now I saw that the word SOLD had been nailed across the real-estate agent's sign. A moving van, with SNIGGLY MOVING COMPANY: WE PROMISE NOT TO BREAK TOO MUCH on the side, was backed into the driveway, and two men were carrying an old canopy bed into the house.

"I guess someone is finally moving in," I said.

"Aw, shoot," Solly said, and scuffed his toe. "I was kind of hoping that Ginger would move back." Just then G.W., Solly's pet rat, peeked his nose out of the pocket sewn into his cape. Solly reached back to stroke G.W.'s head. "Oh, well, maybe some kids are moving in."

"I don't see any bikes," I said. "Or basketballs. Or a toboggan."

"Let's go ask."

Solly started across the road and I followed. The two burly moving men were coming back out of the house. "Excuse me," Solly said. "I don't suppose the person moving in owns an ice-cream parlor?"

"Sorry, kid," said the burlier moving man. "He's a teacher. Going to start teaching in that school over there. His name is – let me see the sheet here."

The mover pulled out a bill that was scrunched in his pocket. "Mr. Parsstinka. Teaches science, I believe."

"I'm getting a new science teacher," I said. "Does he seem strict?"

"Couldn't really tell. Seems a bit nervous, actually. I think maybe it's his first job. Well, we better get to work."

"Thanks," Solly said. "And if you need help lifting a piano or anything, just give Googoo-man a call. I'm in the Yellow Pages."

"Thanks, kid."

We started walking fast so we wouldn't be late.

"You're so lucky," Solly said. "New teachers always bring brownies and let you watch movies and play games."

"I guess so," I said, even though I wasn't so crazy about getting a new teacher.

We reached the school, where kids were crowding in through the doors, talking excitedly.

"What's going on?" I asked Julia Worthington, as we came up behind her.

"We're having an assembly!" Julia said. "Everyone is supposed to go straight to the gym."

"Hey, there's that new boy – the one you think is so cute," Solly said. "Hey, Fox, my sister thinks – *ouch!*"

I had pinched Solly just in time. Fox stopped. He'd enrolled in our school two weeks ago and all that I knew about him, besides his unusual name, was that he had a little scar on his chin from falling off his trike when he was three, that he could play "Chopsticks" on the piano, and that he'd seen about every episode of *The Simpsons*.

Hearing his name, Fox had stopped and turned to look, causing three people to crash into him.

"Don't mind my brother," I said. "I mean, he thinks he's a superhero."

"You're Eleanor, right? We're in the same science class."

"Uh-huh. So where are you going to sit for the assembly?"

"As far back as possible," he said, rolling his eyes. I guess he didn't like assemblies. "You want to –"

But he didn't get to finish because Solly interrupted. "*We* like sitting up front," Solly said, grabbing my arm. "Come on, sis, let's get a good seat."

"But I –"

It was too late. The crowd surged forward, pushing Fox away from us. That was just great – I'd *so* much rather sit with my little brother. We went through the gym doors. Looking ahead at the rows of kids already sitting on the floor, I said, "There's no room up front."

"Sure, there is. Come on."

Solly pulled me by the arm as he stepped between people. "Make way, make way! We're on the Lomox Committee."

It worked. Kids shifted to let us pass. Solly got us right up to the front row, where we squeezed between a couple of younger kids. "The Lomox Committee?" I said.

"*Shh*," Solly hissed, "or you'll be kicked off the committee."

I was going to say something back when Principal Bentham walked in. Mr. Bentham used to be my teacher, but he had been promoted to head of the school. He still had the habit of talking with his eyes closed, only now kids who were in trouble would make faces while he lectured them. He walked up to the microphone at the front of the gym and tapped it several times.

"Hello, hello? Is this working? *Row, row, row your boat . . .* ah, now it's on. Good morning, boys and girls. We have a special assembly today. As you know, we like to bring in people with interesting jobs to speak to you about their careers. Well, the man I'm going to introduce has a very interesting job indeed. In fact, he may be the only person in the world to have this job. He's a creature catcher."

"Oh, please, no," I said.

"Boys and girls, let's give a real Inkpotts-Public-School welcome to Mr. Levon du Plessy-Minsk!"

Applause, foot pounding, and whistles came from the audience. But then, the kids in our school would applaud a speaker if his job was to put the bristles on toilet-bowl brushes.

Levon du Plessy-Minsk was a lot shorter than he looked on television. He wore his pith helmet, hunter's vest, and camouflage pants. His little mustache twitched as he waved to us.

"Well, hello, children," he boomed into the microphone. "I'm sure many of you know who I am. No doubt you are thrilled to see me in person. I know I am. Today I want to tell you about some of my exciting adventures stalking the world's rarest creatures – so rare that many people don't believe they exist. But they do, children, they do!

"For example, take Bigfoot, otherwise known as Sasquatch. Nine feet tall, completely covered with thick hair. Enormous claws and beady black eyes. Some people believe that Bigfoot is a peaceful, shy creature, but I assure you that it is mean, dangerous, and hungry for blood! Why, it's a good thing that I keep in top physical condition, or I wouldn't be here today. Because when you come face-to-face –"

A hand shot up beside me. It was Solly's.

"Put your hand down!" I hissed. "I don't want him to notice us."

But it was too late; Levon du Plessy-Minsk had already seen him. "I spy an eager hand. Excellent. Yes, you, the boy in the interesting costume. Please go ahead."

Solly stood up. He was such a ham! "I read your book about hunting Bigfoot," he said. "It's in the library."

"Very good. I'm so glad you mentioned it because I just happen to have a hundred or so copies that will be for sale after the presentation. Autographed, of course."

"I read your book twice."

"I'm very flattered. You may sit down now."

"I read it twice because I thought that I must have missed something the first time. Because, in the book, you never actually catch Bigfoot. You never even *see* Bigfoot."

"Ah, yes, well, you're a very attentive reader. Do sit down. If I might just hold up the book, everyone will see the picture of the fierce and terrifying Bigfoot on the cover."

"But, Mr. du Plessy-Minsk," Solly persisted, "that's just a *drawing*. There aren't any actual photographs of Bigfoot in the book. There's a photograph of a tree that Bigfoot might want to climb. There's a photograph of a cave where Bigfoot might want to sleep. But there's no Bigfoot. You never found it."

Levon du-Plessy Minsk looked to the side, shaking his head with annoyance. Then he looked back. "All right. I never did find Bigfoot. Are you happy? But it's still a very exciting book. I have many adventures in it. I fall in a hole. I get stung by a bee. There's an amusing episode in which I eat some overripe blackberries and can't find a washroom. It's well worth the money. Now, if I might continue with my lecture. . . ."

"But, Mr. du Plessy-Minsk," Solly said, "I've also read your book on the Loch Ness Monster. It's in the library too."

"Did you? I think it's even better than my book on Bigfoot. There are fewer spelling errors. And a terrible monster it is. Like a swimming dinosaur, with a long neck, humongous teeth, and weighing five thousand pounds."

"But you never saw the Loch Ness Monster either."

Mr. du Plessy-Minsk stopped. He looked at Solly. He took a step forward. "What is your name, young man?"

"It's Solly!" somebody shouted out. I recognized the voice of Julia Worthington's brother, Jeremy. "Solly Blande!"

"Well, Solly Blande, I would have seen it if my boat hadn't sprung a leak and sunk, and if I hadn't got seaweed in my bathing suit, and if the Scottish police hadn't taken me in for trespassing. What exactly is your point?"

Solly looked down at his shoes. He lowered his voice. "It's just that, if you haven't found either of these other creatures, then what makes you think you're going to find the Mysterious Flying Girl? I mean, maybe she's just a myth too. Maybe you shouldn't bother. Maybe you should just forget about it."

Finally Solly sat down. Nobody said a word. In his own crazy way, my brother was a genius. Maybe now this Levon du Plessy-Minsk would leave us alone.

Mr. Bentham came to the front again and tapped on the microphone. "Hello? *Mary had a little* – ah, good. You've made some excellent points, Solly. Perhaps you could use some of that fine thinking in your next school assignments. Yes, skepticism is an essential ingredient to scientific thinking. Perhaps our guest has changed his mind about looking for this flying girl. Have you, Mr. du Plessy-Pinsk?"

Levon du Plessy-Minsk stepped forward to the microphone. "Not Pinsk, Minsk. And, no, I haven't. And I'll tell you why. Because I have proof."

Stirrings in the audience. "Proof?" I said, louder than I meant to.

"Yes, young woman," he said, looking at me. "And what is your name?"

"Eleanor Blande!" shouted Jeremy.

"I see. First your brother, now you. Your whole family is stacked against me, is it? Well, I'll show you proof. Turn down the lights!"

Principal Bentham nodded and the lights dimmed. A moment later, a square of light flickered to life on the gym wall behind Levon du Plessy-Minsk. Everyone hushed. It was a movie, grainy and poorly lit – clearly it had been taken at night. It took me a second to realize that I was looking at a corner of our own school, with the playing field off to the right. A movement caught my attention, something flickering just over the trees at the field's edge.

It grew larger as it skimmed towards the school, turning towards the camera.

It was . . . *me!*

Solly grabbed my arm. We watched as I flew up to the corner of the school and hovered there a moment. I could recognize my pajamas, but it was too dark and blurry to make out my face. A second later I shot past the camera, which turned shakily and caught me going off in the other direction. I grew smaller and smaller until I disappeared. The movie ended and the lights went on.

Levon du Plessy-Minsk stood before us, grinning broadly. He raised his hands like a rock star. "You see? You see! There *is* a Mysterious Flying Girl. That film was taken by the camera on my minivan just three days ago. It is proof positive that she exists. Not only that, but she has flown over your own school! It is therefore my opinion that she lives in this very neighborhood."

Even the teachers gasped. "That's right," he said. "She might live on your street. She might even be a student at this school. In fact, she just might be sitting beside you!"

Everyone looked around. A few kids laughed nervously.

Principal Bentham stepped forward again and tapped on the microphone. "Hello? *Twinkle, twinkle* . . . right, then. That was a most interesting presentation. Now we must continue on with our day. After all, at Inkpotts Public School, we are here to learn, learn, learn. However, Mr. du Plessy-Minsk has kindly agreed to sign copies of his books for purchase. You may line up in the hallway outside. Everyone else, please go to your classrooms."

Everyone stood up. Solly and I did too, but we felt too stunned to speak. As we made our way through the crowd, Julia Worthington came up to us.

"Hey, Eleanor," Julia said. "It isn't you, is it?"

"Me?"

"Just kidding. But I bet he's right. I bet it's someone in our very own school. And he's going to catch her. Are you coming to buy a book?"

"I don't think so," I said. But she had already rushed ahead to get into line.

COLD
FEET

After dinner, we were all sitting around the living room. Mom looked up from the travel book she was reading and said, "I've been thinking about our summer vacation. We could fly over the Great Wall of China. Wouldn't that be something?"

"I don't see what's so great about a wall," Solly said. He was lying on the rug, playing with G.W. "A floor, maybe. A ceiling, possibly. An ancient toilet, definitely. But a wall?"

"Thank you for that thoughtful response," Mom said. "If you want to see an ancient toilet, we should go to Pompeii. What do you think, Eleanor?"

"Oh, whatever."

"What's the matter, honey? Are you thinking about that creature-catching person? Levon du Plessy-Minsk?"

"It's kind of spooking me out. I don't understand why he wants to catch me anyway."

"I guess it makes him feel important. But don't worry. If you don't fly, he can't catch you, right?"

As if that was a great solution! Here I was, with the permanent mark of a quarter moon and three stars on my palm, which meant that I could fly whenever I wanted, and I couldn't fly at all.

"Anyway, let's say he does catch you," Solly said. "And you get put in the zoo. Would that be so bad? You get all the peanuts you want. And you don't have to take math. And we could visit you every month."

"Stop that," Dad said. He was sitting in an old stained T-shirt and sweatpants, his mandolin in his lap. One of the strings had broken and he was supposed to change it, but he just held it in his lap, as if he didn't have the energy.

Solly's jokes were getting on my nerves. He liked to fly too, but he didn't seem to miss it as much as I did. That overheated imagination kept him busy enough.

The doorbell rang.

"Probably some fans of Googoo-man," Solly said. "Tell them I'm not signing autographs today."

"Yeah," I said, "because his sister duct-taped his hands to the refrigerator."

"How about I tell them that Googoo-man needs to get in the bath?" Mom said, getting up. I could hear her open the front door and then the sound of her voice greeting someone. A moment later, she was ushering a man into the room. He was tall, with graying hair swept to the sides, and wore a black suit with a crest on it. In his hand, he held a silver envelope, and he looked at me and smiled. Now I recognized him! It was His Excellency H. Waldorf Mansfield, the ambassador of Verulia.

We had first met him in the fortress on Mount Darkling in Verulia, where he was a captain in Kaspar Snit's warrior army. But he had only been there by force; he'd really wanted to be a ballet dancer. The last time we had seen him was to hand over the one million dollars that kids from all over had sent in to help rebuild Verulia after the earthquake.

"Wally!" I said, jumping up. That was what he liked us to call him. He came forward and gave me a hug, then he hugged Solly too.

"It's so wonderful to see you all," he said. "I have a tear in my eye. I'm such a softy! And you have all been such good friends to Verulia. That million dollars has helped us to rebuild our schools and hospitals."

"That's really great to hear," Dad said. "You kids should be proud."

"Did you put in a waterslide park, like I suggested?" Solly asked.

"Not yet, I'm afraid," said Wally. "However, we do hope to make our country more beautiful now that everything is in working order. But I've almost forgotten the reason I'm here. It's to give you this." He held the silver envelope out to my parents.

Dad took it and turned it over for us to see the Verulian coat of arms on one side. Then he opened it carefully and pulled out the square of heavy cream-colored paper, which he held out for all of us to read. The words were printed in gold ink.

H. Waldorf Mansfield, ambassador of Verulia
requests your presence at the opening ceremony
for the new exhibit

ANCIENT SPLENDOR:
GOLD, SILVER, JEWELRY, AND OTHER
VALUABLE STUFF FROM THE
STATE TREASURES OF VERULIA

at the Constance Foote Museum of Art,
April 16, 7:00 P.M.

"How exciting," Mom said. "We'll be thrilled to go."

"I'm so glad to hear it," Wally said. "The people of Verulia consider the Blande family our most special friends. You will be honored guests at the opening, I assure you. We're bringing our most rare and beautiful objects. Crowns, scepters, diamonds, carvings, and the most spectacular object of all: the gold sarcophagus of the last ancient king. We're hoping the exhibit will be a big success. The money from ticket sales will be used to beautify Verulia's cities and towns."

"Well," Dad said, rubbing his chin, "I guess I'm going to have to shave for the opening."

"And I'm going to iron my cape," Solly said.

"Splendid," said Wally. "Now, if you'll excuse me, I just arrived from Verulia an hour ago. There are only two weeks to the opening and my life is going to be awfully hectic. But I will see you on April 16th!"

Wally gave us the official Verulian bow and then he hugged us again. He even hugged Dad, who wasn't looking very huggable these days. We all went to the door and watched him walk to his waiting limousine. He did a quick pirouette and got in. As the limo pulled away, he rolled down the window and waved to us. We all waved back.

"I bet he has a television in that limo," Solly said. "With cable."

After Solly had his bath, I took a shower and went to bed and read for a while. Then I turned out the light, but I couldn't sleep. I listened for the sound of my parents' voices. Usually, I could hear them talking quietly, but tonight they were silent. I knew that my mom was worried about my dad. Of course, she was worried about him not having work, which meant that the family had less money, but I could tell she was more worried that he seemed to have given up. My dad had been so dedicated to fountains for so many years that I was sure he must feel lost without any fountain work. When I asked Mom about it the other night, she said that Dad needed us to be patient and supportive until he became himself again.

I turned over in bed. This was one of those nights when I felt that, if I didn't fly, I would burst out of my skin. I knew that it was a risk with Levon du Plessy-Minsk on the prowl, but if I was careful to keep a sharp lookout and not to go near the school, I figured that I could avoid him. So I got up, carefully opened my door, and crept down the dark hallway to the living room.

And saw a dark form standing by the window. Mom.

The window was open, and Mom was standing before it in her tracksuit and running shoes. It was only a couple of days since she had taken an imprint from my hand, so I knew that she could fly. The ancient amulet that my great-great-grandmother had found on her travels had been lost when a pigeon flew off with it from inside Misery Mountain. But the imprint of its raised pattern – a quarter moon and three stars – had remained permanently on my own palm. As Mom said, "You're our amulet now, Eleanor." If Mom or Solly or even Dad wanted to fly, they had to get the imprint from me. So I knew that she could fly, but I was surprised that she was going to, considering the stern warning that she and Dad had given to us.

But there she was – hands at her sides, feet apart, chin up. But she looked different than usual. It took me a moment to realize that she was breathing hard, her arms were trembling, and her face didn't have the usual happy, expectant look.

Rivetted to the doorway, I watched Mom rise on her toes, lower herself, and rise again, as if she were struggling against some invisible force. *What could it be?* Suddenly she said, "I can't!" and stepped backwards. Her arms went limp and she took several deep breaths, like she was about to faint.

"Mom?"

She turned and saw me in the doorway. A look passed over her face – like she wasn't so glad to see me – but then she smiled and waved me over. I hurried toward her, but then felt shy and just stood close by, not knowing what to do.

"Are you okay?" I said.

Mom sighed. She led me to the sofa, where we sat down beside each other. She looked into my eyes. "I was trying to hide it from you, but I guess I can't anymore," she said. "It's just that . . . well . . . I can't fly."

"You can't? Did the imprint fade already?"

"No, it's still there."

"Then why can't you fly?"

"Because I'm afraid to."

"I don't get it. You've flown a million times – way before I even knew about it. How can you be afraid?"

"I don't know, Eleanor. It came on me slowly. I began to feel a little nervous right before lifting off. Then the nervousness grew. I'd start to feel dizzy just thinking about flying. And a couple of weeks ago, I couldn't get myself to rise up. I've developed a fear of flying."

"But you've always loved to fly, just like me."

"I know. I miss it, but I can't do it."

"What exactly are you afraid of, Mom? That you're going to suddenly fall out of the sky? Or smash into something?"

"It's not as specific as that. It's just . . . well . . . fear."

I looked into Mom's eyes, took her hand, and squeezed it. Then I thought of something that grown-ups sometimes say. "Maybe you need professional help."

Mom laughed a little. "Yes, probably. But do you think there's a psychiatrist around who specializes in helping people who fly?"

I laughed too. We sat for a moment without speaking. *How weird was this?* First my dad began moping around the house, not getting dressed, irritating everyone. And now Mom couldn't fly. I had thought that nothing could ever go wrong with my parents. It was their job to fix the things that went wrong with *us*. And here they both were, needing – but what *did* they need?

"Are you two getting some fresh air?"

It was Dad. He stood in the doorway, where I had been a few moments before, looking at us with his hands on his hips.

"Manfred," Mom said, sounding embarrassed. "What are you doing up?"

"I had a feeling there might be some irresponsible activity tonight. I thought I should check up. Are you all right, Daisy?"

He stepped towards us and I could see, by the way he looked at Mom, that he already knew about her problem. He didn't sound mad, despite the warning he'd given us. He took Mom's hand. "You look like you need some sleep," he said. "Why don't you go back to bed? I'll sit up with Eleanor awhile."

"All right," she said. She gave us both a tired smile. "Don't stay up too late, you two." Dad and I watched her walk slowly out of the dark room. Then we heard the bedroom door shut gently down the hall.

"Poor Mom," Dad said. "I've never seen her like this."

The thought came to me: *I've never seen either of you like this,* but I didn't say it out loud. Instead I said, "Dad, I really need to fly. Can't I go for a short ride? I'll be super careful."

Dad put his hand on my shoulder. He was wearing the cowboy pajamas that Solly and I had given him for his birthday. "If you really need to fly, Eleanor, I would feel safer if you had company."

"You mean, you'll come with me? But you never fly just for the fun of it."

"There's a first time for everything. The only problem is," he said, turning over his hand, "that I'm out of gas. Would you mind filling me up?"

"Very good, sir."

I lifted my own hand and put my palm against Dad's. We pressed them together for a long moment and then let go. When Dad lifted his hand, we could see the imprint of the quarter moon and stars.

"Okay, captain," Dad said, "let's go. But take it easy. I'm not a natural talent like you are."

Dad stepped aside to give me room at the window and I got into position. I closed my eyes and, almost before I had a chance to think about being light, I felt a breeze touch my face. When I opened my eyes, I was hovering in the dark over the house. Dad was looking up at me through the window. He gave me the thumbs-up sign and got into position. I could see that his hands were not at the right angle, but before I had a chance to call down he started to rise, spinning as he went up.

"*Whoa!*" Dad said, whirling past me. "*Ouch, ouch, ouch!*" He scraped on the branches of the tree above.

"Are you all right?" I said, coming up beside him.

"Just a little rusty. Lead the way, Eleanor. And let's both keep a lookout."

I knew Dad wasn't keen on getting too high or going too fast, so we flew just over the trees, past the community-center tennis courts and along streets, keeping an eye out for a white minivan. Even though I liked to go higher and faster, it was nice to have Dad's company, so I didn't mind. Feeling the urge, I swooped up and then did a loop down again.

"Is that supposed to be fun?" Dad said, as I fell back in beside him.

"It *is* fun. You should try it."

"Call me crazy, but I prefer not to be upside down when I'm flying. Look, there's Rooster's Fried Chicken. I have a craving for fast food. Feel like having an order of triple-fried nuggets? It's open twenty-four hours."

"Sure, Dad, as long as we don't tell Mom."

"You got that right."

Mom always said that Rooster's was worse than other fast-food restaurants. I wondered if Dad was really hungry or just wanted a break. He wasn't exactly in top shape, since he'd been sitting around in his bathrobe every day. But I didn't mind the thought of a Rooster's chocolate sludge sundae. We circled around and headed towards the empty parking lot. I glanced over at my father.

"Dad," I called, "you're going in too fast!"

"Now you tell me?"

Dad's feet touched the ground at too high a speed. He had to run on his bare feet so as not to fall down. *"Yeeaow!"* he cried, grabbing on to the pole of a parking sign. He spun around the pole, his arms and legs winding around it, until he scraped to a stop.

I landed beside him. "Are you okay?"

"Me? I'm perfectly fine. But now I'm really hungry," he said. "We can go to the drive-through window and eat outside on the bench. It's such a nice night. Plus, that way, they won't see that we're in our pajamas. Good thing I stuck a few dollars in my pocket."

It was funny, but now I was feeling hungry too. I decided on fries, with that sundae, and told my dad. Then we went up to the drive-through window.

"I bet you never went to a restaurant in the middle of the night," Dad said. "See? Your old pops can be adventurous too." The sliding window had a rectangle of plywood over it so that we couldn't see inside. Dad rang the buzzer. We were startled by a crashing sound. There was a long pause and then the sound of a key turning in a lock. The window slid open.

A man's face appeared. He was kind of hard to see because he was wearing a ski hat and sunglasses, with several bandages on his chin.

"What happened to you?" Dad said.

"Ah, I fell into the milkshake machine," the man croaked.

"That's got to hurt," I said.

"Well, what do you want?"

"We'd like an order of triple-fried nuggets, an order of famous fatty fries, a chocolate sludge sundae, and a lurid lime soda, please," Dad said.

"We're out of nuggets."

"Two orders of fries then."

"We're out of fries too."

"Then just the drink and the sundae."

"We're out of both."

"Have you got anything to eat or drink?"

"I've got water, but it isn't very clean. Now go away."

The window slammed shut.

"That's no way to run a business," Dad said, with a shrug. "Oh, well, we'll just have to fly hungry."

Something didn't seem right about the man in the window, but before I could say anything, I heard the awful screeching of tires. We turned to see a white minivan braking in the parking lot. It slammed to a halt, shaking as if it would throw off all its parts. Then the driver's door swung open and the driver fell out.

"Did you see them? Did you see them?" cried the man, struggling to get up and pushing his pith helmet out of his eyes.

Pith helmet? It was Levon du Plessy-Minsk!

He tried to get up, but tripped over the pole of a large butterfly net he was holding. "They were right up there!" he said.

"I'm sorry, but we don't know what you're talking about," Dad said.

"In the air! Not one, but two! Flying! Actually flying! I would have had it all on camera if I hadn't forgotten to take the lens cap off. They landed right here; I saw them from the highway."

Finally he got to his feet and hurried up to us, his eyes gleaming. "I'm *this* close," he said, holding up two pinched fingers, "I can feel it. Are you sure you didn't see anything?"

"Not a thing," I said, with a gulp.

He squinted one eye suspiciously at me. "Wait a minute. I recognize you from the school. Eleanor Blande, right?"

"Yes," I said.

"And I'm her father, Manfred Blande," Dad said.

"You're wearing pajamas. What are you doing in your pajamas?"

"An excellent question. Isn't it, Eleanor?"

"Sure. It's a first-rate question."

"And now we'll say good night," Dad said.

"Wait! You haven't answered it."

"We haven't? How silly of us. Eleanor, answer the question."

Why did Dad always make me answer these impossible questions? "Okay," I said, stalling for time. "It's . . . um . . . it's because of moths."

"Moths?"

"Yes. Giant moths from Brazil. They ate all our clothes, didn't they, Dad?"

"Right down to our socks. Pesky insects."

"But why didn't they eat your pajamas?"

"They were saving our pajamas for dessert," I said. "We got them away just in time."

"Well," Dad sighed, "it's long past this young lady's bedtime. So we'll say good night again."

We turned away and I breathed a sigh of relief. But then I heard Levon du Plessy-Minsk's voice behind us. "Hold on, there. You don't have a car. The parking lot's empty. Don't tell me the moths ate your car too."

"Oh, that's very droll," Dad said, pretending to chuckle. "The moths ate our car! Did you hear that, Eleanor?"

"I did."

"Tell the good man what happened to our car."

"Sure. Actually, it got towed. By the police."

"Sad but true," Dad said.

"Why did the police tow your car away?"

"Punishment," I answered brightly. "For importing giant moths from Brazil."

"It's illegal," Dad said, with a shrug. "On account of their taste for clothes."

"But they were so cute," I added.

"Adorable. And now we've got a long walk ahead of us. *Toot-a-loo.*"

"Wait," Levon du Plessy-Minsk said. "I can give you a lift in my minivan."

"Is it safe?" Dad asked.

"Perfectly safe. I superglued the side panels on myself."

"But it's far too much trouble."

"No trouble at all. I need someone to show my map to anyway."

"Map?"

"Yes, my map of all the sightings of the Mysterious Flying Girl. It shows a very interesting pattern."

Dad and I turned and looked at each other. "All right," Dad said quietly. "We'll take a look at your map."

A STAMP
AND AN
ICE CREAM

Levon du Plessy-Minsk led the way to the minivan and ushered us in through the back doors. We could see tracking and recording equipment all along the walls. There were also night-vision goggles, Geiger counters, powerful flashlights, and gauges showing wind direction, air pressure, and temperature. We put on seat belts as Levon du Plessy-Minsk turned the key, making the engine cough as if it had a bad cold.

Dad told him our address.

"Perfect," he said, as the minivan pulled away. "That happens to be just the neighborhood I'm going to. So tell me, Mr. Blande, what do you do?"

Dad hesitated, perhaps because he didn't feel like he did much of anything. But then he said, "I'm a fountain expert."

"A fountain expert? There's a weird job."

Weirder than a creature catcher? I thought.

Levon du Plessy Minsk went on, "I'm glad I ran into someone who knows the neighborhood well. I'm on the verge of a breakthrough. I came close today – really, I don't know how they got away. Next time, I'll get that Mysterious Flying Girl and whoever else she's with. Who knows, there might be a colony of flying people . . . a secret civilization. They might be trying to take over the world. Catching them will be a service to all normal, nonflying humanity. One day, a national holiday might even be declared in my honor. My face could be on a postage stamp. Ben and Jerry will name an ice cream after me."

"Yeah," whispered my dad, "and it'll be full of nuts."

I giggled. A few minutes later, the minivan pulled up in front of our house. "Well, thanks for the ride," Dad said, starting to open the door. "We'll see you."

"Wait!" Levon du Plessy-Minsk turned around in his seat. "I haven't shown you the map." He climbed into the back, Dad and I ducking his flying arms and legs, and pulled down a rolled-up map. Then he picked up a pointer and tapped it on one of the dozen or so red *X*'s on it. "All theses *X*'s show a Mysterious Flying Girl sighting," he said. "Notice the interesting spiral pattern from these farthest ones, which are quite scattered, towards this concentration right over your neighborhood. Three over the school. Two over the park. Three more right on your street. Quite a few of them were called in by a fellow named Worthington. What do you make of it?"

"Did you say Worthington?" Dad asked.

"I did."

"That's too bad."

"What do you mean?"

"I know Mr. Worthington very well," Dad said. "An upstanding citizen. Unfortunately, his eyesight isn't very good."

"It isn't?"

"He refuses to wear glasses. He even denies that he needs them. Isn't that right, Eleanor?"

"Yes, that's right. Remember, Dad, that time he thought there was a pterodactyl in his backyard?"

"I do. It was just Solly's radio-controlled aeroplane. We all had a good laugh over that one."

"And the time he fell in a manhole and the fire department had to get him out? And the time he accidentally got into a helicopter, thinking it was a taxi . . . ?"

"That's enough examples, Eleanor," Dad said, giving me a look.

"This is very disappointing, very *very* disappointing," Levon du Plessy-Minsk said. "I really thought I was on to something."

Dad patted him on the shoulder. "Don't worry. I'm sure you'll find an interesting creature one day. A centaur. A werewolf. You keep at it, Mr. du Plessy-Minsk. Perhaps you'll have better luck somewhere else."

Dad opened a back door and we hopped out. We stood in the dark beside our fountain and watched the minivan slowly pull away.

Dad said, "A helicopter?"

"I guess I got carried away."

Dad chuckled, which made me laugh, and into the house we went.

WELCOME,
MR. PARSSTINKA

"I don't want a new science teacher," I said. "I want Mrs. Doovis back."

"I know you do," Mom said, sliding some scrambled eggs onto my plate. "But she has to take care of her new baby."

"I think she should bring her baby to class," Dad said, pouring the orange juice. As usual, he wore his bathrobe. "Now *that* would be an education."

"What's your new teacher's name again?" Mom said.

"Mr. Parsstinka."

"Pretty funny name," Solly said, his mouth full of eggs, which was a revolting sight. "I mean Par-*sstink*-a? It'll be so easy to make fun of him. *'Excuse me, Mr. Parsstinka, o you?'* Or, how about, '*Mr. Parsstinka needs to wash he sinka.'*"

"That's enough," Dad said. "He probably comes from another country. His name might mean something perfectly nice. Making fun of foreign names is acting prejudiced."

"I don't care what his name is, as long as he's not horrible. He's going to be my homeroom teacher too."

"Remember last year," Mom said, "when you didn't want Mrs. Leer to be your nanny? And now we all can't wait for her to visit. You two better hurry up. Manfred, have you got any work today?"

"No," he sighed. "The town of Meaford was thinking of putting in a fountain, but decided on a new traffic light instead."

She kissed Dad on the cheek. "I'm sure things will turn around. There's a shopping list on the fridge. Now hustle, you two."

Solly and I walked to school. Lost in my thoughts, it took me a while to notice that Solly wasn't chattering away as usual. In fact, he was practically dragging his feet, his goggled eyes staring at the ground.

"What's wrong with you?" I said.

"I don't know. I guess I'm feeling discouraged."

"About what?"

"For one thing, I don't have a new best friend. I mean, I play with Jeremy next door and other kids too, but none of them is as fun as Ginger Hirshbein. Once, Ginger put on a bathing suit, covered his entire body in shaving cream, and walked down the street introducing himself as Mr. Foamy. It doesn't get better than that."

"I admit you were a good match. That's rough."

"And second of all, I don't know if I want to be Googoo-man anymore."

"What?" I stopped and looked at Solly.

He looked back at me and then at the ground, where he kicked a stone with his shoe. I could see that he wasn't joking.

"What do you mean? You've been Googoo-man since you were six years old."

"Exactly. Don't you think I'm a little bit old to be wearing this outfit? When I was little, I thought it looked totally cool. But now it just looks goofy. Not to mention, I don't really have any superpowers, except for flying, and if I tried to rescue people from a burning building or to stop a gang of robbers, Mom and Dad would ground me until I was thirty. I mean, I'm not really a superhero. I'm a nine-year-old kid with a *C+* average who spends most of his time playing with a rodent. Being Googoo-man is just stupid. It's time to hang up my goggles."

"But if you aren't Googoo-man," I said, "then who are you?"

"That's what I'd like to know."

Solly began walking again, dragging his feet like before, his cape hanging like a defeated flag around his neck. I had always been embarrassed by his ridiculous outfit and I had often wished that he would dress like everybody else. But the truth was, I couldn't imagine Solly *not* being Googoo-man.

First, my dad lost his work. Then my mom became afraid to fly. Now Solly was having an identity crisis. *Could there be anybody else who needed help?*

I hurried to catch up. "This is not something to make a quick decision about," I said. "I mean, it's big. It's huge. You might feel differently about it tomorrow."

"I've been feeling this way for weeks. But I've kept it up because I don't want to disappoint all of Googoo-man's admirers. And then, you know what? I realized that Googoo-man doesn't have any admirers."

"Yes, he does," I said quickly. "Me."

"Really?"

"Okay, not always. But I'd miss Googoo-man if he wasn't here, as much as I hate to admit it. Just hang in there awhile."

"I guess I'll think about. Well, see you after school, Eleanor."

We had reached the edge of the school grounds and headed for the doors, where the last kids were straggling in. Solly went along the hall while I headed up the stairs to the second floor. Everyone was hurrying to class. I didn't want to be late for homeroom so I hurried too, my anxiety about the new teacher returning. But when I got to class, the new teacher hadn't arrived yet and kids were hopping about like mad. Some were leaping over desks playing tag, while others were shooting crumpled science assignments at the garbage can they'd put up on the teacher's desk. Some girls at the front were learning dance moves from Julia Worthington, and other kids were drawing all over the blackboard.

The only person who wasn't acting crazy was the boy named Fox. He was sitting at his desk, hunched over a piece of paper. He had streaky hair that fell over his eyes and wore red running shoes, as always.

"What are you doing?" I asked, sitting down at my own desk.

Fox looked up, his face frowning with concentration. "Drawing."

"Can I see?"

"Only if you don't say anything mean."

"I'll try not to."

He leaned back so that I could see the paper on the desk. It was a pencil drawing of a horse. Or, half a horse – the front half – and just the outline of the back. It was pretty good, although I thought the ears were too big.

"Not bad," I said.

"The head's not quite right. And the ears. Oh, well." He crumpled up the paper and quickly tossed it towards the garbage can on the teacher's desk. It hit the rim and bounced off. "I'm not much good at basketball either," he said. "So what are you good at?"

"I'm pretty good at flying." *Oh no, had I really said that out loud?*

"Flying?" he said, looking at me. "You can, uh, fly?"

"No, no, of course I can't fly. Yeah, right. Zoom-zoom, here I go. No, I meant flieing, spelled *F-L-I-E-I-N-G*. It's totally different."

"Okay, so what's flieing?"

How did I get myself into this? "Well, it's hard to explain. Flieing means 'falling' and 'lying.' You have to fall and tell a lie at the same time."

"Gee, that sounds like a handy talent. You'll have to show me."

"Well, it's better outdoors –"

The slamming of the door gave me an excuse to shut up. It was Principal Bentham, who leaned on the teacher's desk, his eyes already closing. "All right, people, do please settle down now. We aren't studying the barbarian invasions, are we? Everyone, go to your seats."

Principal Bentham was known to be a softy, and everyone took their time sitting down. "We don't want to make a poor first impression on your new homeroom and science teacher, do we? Now, students, before Mr. Parsstinka comes in, I want you to know that he has no doubt heard every joke imaginable about his name. And now, boys and girls, I'd like you to welcome your new teacher."

Mr. Bentham opened the door. There was a pause, and then a man stepped into the classroom. He was tall, well groomed, with a curling mustache and a black cape. He looked at us with a dark glint in his eye.

"So these are my new students," he purred. "How very delightful."

Our new teacher was . . . Kaspar Snit.

THE GENUINE
SWORN AFFIDAVIT

Principal Bentham slipped out, closing the door behind him. Quickly I wrote the teacher's name on the back of my notebook: *P-A-R-S-S-T-I-N-K-A*. As I silently spelled Kaspar Snit, I crossed out each letter. Yup, sure enough, the letters matched.

How could this possibly happen? How could I end up with an evil genius for my homeroom teacher? He could do anything he wanted. We were all defenseless.

"Good morning, class," Kaspar Snit said, his mouth curling up at one end. It didn't seem as if he'd spotted me, and I slouched down lower in my seat. "It's true that I am a new teacher and that this is my very first class. But that doesn't mean I'm a pushover. Together we are going to learn about the wonders of science. I'm sure

41

we'll have a few bumps along the way, getting to know one another, but it will all smooth out. Now, will somebody please tell me what you were working on with your last teacher?"

Kaspar Snit stared at us. I was sure that, no matter what anyone said, he would have a nasty reply. But nobody put a hand up – not even Julia Worthington, who was always squealing with impatience to be picked.

"You're feeling a little shy, are you?" Kaspar Snit said. "That's understandable. Why don't I just call on someone? I've got the class list right here. I'll just run my finger down the names and stop at one. Here we are. ELEANOR BLANDE. Can you tell us what you're studying, Ms. Blande?"

Kaspar Snit looked over the heads of the students, as if waiting for someone to identify herself. Reluctantly, I stood up. When he saw me, he didn't show any sign of knowing who I was, but smiled in a ghastly, if encouraging, sort of way.

"Combustion," I said. "We're studying combustion."

"A favorite topic of mine. And can you define combustion for us, Ms. Blande?"

"Things burning, I guess."

"Close enough. And can you think of a human invention that makes use of combustion?"

"I'm blanking out," I said.

"No matter. How about the internal combustion engine? Without it, we would not have invented cars. Or aeroplanes, for that matter. That's right, Ms. Blande, without the internal combustion engine, the Wright Brothers would not have been able to fly. I don't suppose you can think of a way of flying that doesn't require an engine?"

"Ah, no."

"I didn't think so. You may sit down now."

I didn't exactly sit down; I collapsed into my seat.

Next to me, Fox whispered, "Are you okay? You look like you might throw up. Are you going to throw up? If you're just pretending to be sick, then you're really good at it."

I nodded, but I didn't say anything. I was afraid that if I did, I really would be sick.

When the bell went, I headed for my next class. All day long I could hardly concentrate and, at the end of the day, I rushed over to the basketball net to wait for Solly. Impatiently, I watched the other kids stream out. *Why did Solly always have to be the last?* Finally he appeared, humming his theme song to himself. He didn't sound like he was enjoying it much; he sounded like he was *trying* to enjoy it. But I couldn't worry about Solly's Googoo-man issues now. I had bigger news.

"Solly," I said, "you're not going to believe who my new teacher is."

"I know, Mr. Parsstinka, which rhymes with 'finka.' Let's go home. I want to change out of my Googoo-man outfit. It just feels too dumb."

"Listen to me. My new teacher is –"

"I mean, what am I, seven years old? No. Eight years old? Uh-uh. I'm nine. In some countries, you can get your driver's license when you're nine."

43

"No, you can't."

"Yes, you can. Ginger Hirshbein told me that once."

"Ginger also told you that if you eat enough vanilla ice cream, your hair will turn white."

"Well, have you ever tried?"

"Solly, I'm trying to tell you something."

"Who's stopping you? What's so important anyway? Just tell me already."

"Fine. My new teacher is Kaspar Snit. Now let's go home."

Solly didn't budge. His eyes grew wide and then narrow with suspicion. "Good one, Elly baby. You almost had me believing you. Kaspar Snit teaching at Inkpotts Public School. Let's try that on Mom and Dad and see if we can fool them."

Just then the school doors swung open. Solly and I turned to look. Out came Mr. Parsstinka, otherwise known as Kaspar Snit, in black cape and black fedora, the kind of hat worn by gangsters in old movies. As he strode by, he saw us standing there and tipped his hat without stopping.

"Don't forget to do your homework, Ms. Blande," he said. "We just might have a pop quiz!"

He went to the bicycle rack and undid the lock on a heavy black bike. He mounted it with some difficulty, his knees sticking far out, rang his bell, and wobbled off down the road.

Solly looked at me. "That's the scariest thing I've ever seen."

"You mean seeing Kaspar Snit again?"

"No, I mean watching him try to ride that bike."

Solly and I ran all the way home, flew through the door, and hurried down the hall. I didn't usually let my brother into my room these days – he was always messing up my stuff – but this was an emergency.

"Just think about it," Solly said, picking up a little glass horse from my desk. "Sometimes you get a teacher who's a genius. Sometimes you get one who is evil. But an evil genius? I mean, what are the chances?"

"This is bigger than the two of us," I said, taking the glass horse away from him. "We've got to tell Mom and Dad."

"I agree," he said, picking up my favorite seashell and scraping the edge of it against his chin, like he was shaving. "The only problem is, they won't believe you. I didn't."

"How can we convince them?" I asked, taking away the shell.

"I know," Solly said, putting his sticky hands on my music box. He started to wind the key. "We can write out a sworn affidavit."

"What's a sworn affidavit? And, by the way, if you don't stop winding that key, you're going to break the music box and regret it the rest of your life."

He stopped winding it. "I've seen it on TV shows. It means you swear that something is true. It's an official document."

That sounded like a good idea, so I took out a fresh piece of lined paper and, with Solly helping me to compose, wrote it out.

GENUINE SWORN AFFIDAVIT

We, the undersigned, do swear that, having seen him with our own four eyes, we can positively declare that Mr. Parsstinka, the new teacher at Inkpotts Public School, is none other than the notorious evil genius, Kaspar Snit.

Also, that he's not very good at riding a bicycle.

Signed,
Solly (Saul) Galinski Blande, otherwise known as Googoo-man
Eleanor Galinski Blande

Solly had insisted on the bicycle line. He also thought the affidavit would look more official if it had a red seal on it, but we weren't allowed to light a candle and melt wax, so I chewed a piece of scented cherry bubble gum and stuck it on the paper below our signatures.

It was pretty hard not blurting our news to Dad while he was making fried calamari for dinner, or to Mom, when she got home. Although Solly did forget about Kaspar Snit for a moment, when Mom talked about her day at the passport office where a man wanted to get a passport for his German shepherd. "Wouldn't a German shepherd have to get a German passport?" Solly asked.

Finally dinner was over and Solly and I had to sweep up the kitchen. When we came into the living room, Mom and Dad were talking.

"I don't know what else to do, Daisy," Dad was saying. "I've contacted all my old clients. I've made proposals. There's just no fountain work out there. If this keeps up, we're going to fall behind on our mortgage payments. And we'll have to forget about taking a vacation this summer."

"Maybe, in the meantime," Mom said, "you could do some other kind of work."

"What other kind? Fountains are all I know."

"Well, you could work in a shoe store."

"I don't know anything about shoes. I've been wearing the same pair for five years."

"Or in an office."

"Have you seen how disorganized my own office is?"

"There must be something. I mean, look at you, Manfred. You haven't shaved. You haven't even gotten dressed. Our own fountain is a mess. It's not just for the money. It's unhealthy for you to stay like this. I'm worried about you."

"Don't be worried," Dad said, glancing at a page of the newspaper. But Mom still looked worried.

Solly pushed me forward. "Go on," he said.

"Stop pushing."

"What is it, kids?" Mom said.

"Eleanor has something to give you."

"Maybe it's not a good time," I said.

"Why wouldn't it be a good time? What is it, Eleanor?"

Solly pushed me again. I held out the paper. "Here," I said.

Mom took it from me, smiling as if I were handing her a poem I'd written. "'Genuine Sworn Affidavit,'" she read aloud. The rest she read silently, her mouth slowly turning down.

"Manfred, read this."

"I want to finish this article about a new sport using vacuum cleaners."

"You better read it now."

Dad sighed, but he took the paper from her. Then he sniffed it. "Is that cherry-scented bubble gum?" he said. "This document looks quite realistic. You've done a very good job. The next thing we know, you'll show us your 'genuine' graduation certificates from medical school."

"Dad," I said, "it's not a joke. Kaspar Snit really is my teacher. He's moved into Ginger Hirshbein's old house. He's going to do something awful!"

"Aren't you taking this joke a bit far, Eleanor?" Mom said. "It's good to know when enough is enough –"

Just then the doorbell rang. "I hope it's not that Levon du Plessy-Minsk," Mom said. "When is he going to stop snooping around the neighborhood?"

Dad put aside the newspaper and got up with determination. "I'll tell him he isn't welcome at this house."

"I'll come too, Dad," Solly said. "In case he takes a swing at you."

"He's not going to take a swing at me."

"I'm coming too," I said. "In case he tries to kick Solly."

"Well, if you're all going," Mom said, "I better join you. After all, I did take that seven-week self-defense course."

"Remember, Mom," Solly said, "how you were showing Dad what you learned and you accidentally gave him a black eye?"

"I'd rather we don't talk about it," Dad said, as we approached the door. "Anyway, I can defend myself." He opened the door.

There stood Kaspar Snit, holding his black fedora in his hands. "I hope I am not disturbing you," he said.

"No, no, not at all," Dad stuttered, "we . . . we were just . . . Kaspar Snit?"

"A surprise, no doubt, and not necessarily a happy one for you. But I have come to invite you to dinner."

"Dinner?" Mom said.

"This Saturday evening, at six o'clock. I do hope you can come."

"We'll have to check our calendar," Dad said. "I think we may already be going to dinner at our cousin's house."

"Remember, that got canceled, Dad? They've all got chicken pox."

Dad gave Solly a look. "Oh, yes, thanks for reminding me."

"Then I can expect you?" Kaspar Snit said, with a grimace. "Very good. It is the house just across the road and two doors down. And now I will say good evening."

He put on his hat, turned on his heel, and began to walk away. Passing our fountain, he paused and, without turning his head, reached up and plucked off the plastic bag caught on the horse's ear, stuffing it into his pocket. We watched him turn at the sidewalk, cross the street, and open the door of his own house, closing it behind him.

In the morning, the first thing that my parents did was to march into Principal Bentham's office with Solly and me in tow.

Mr. Bentham was making the last morning announcements into the microphone on his desk: ". . . and so we congratulate our soccer team for trying their hardest, even though they lost yesterday's game seventeen to nothing. Just a reminder that tomorrow is Crazy Hat Day at Inkpotts Public School. And finally, if I might quote the great English poet Robert Browning, may you spend the day picking up learning's crumbs. Have a fairly good day, everyone."

Mr. Bentham switched off the microphone and turned to us. "Daisy, Manfred, I haven't seen you in school for a while. Have you come about the fun fair? Because I want to assure you, there will be no fishpond with live piranhas this year."

"No, Principal Bentham," Dad said. "We haven't come about the fun fair. We've come about Eleanor's new teacher."

"Ah, yes. Mr. Parsstinka. I understand that his first day went very well."

"But his name isn't really Parsstinka," Mom said. "It's –"

"I know," whispered Principal Bentham. "It's Kaspar Snit."

"You know?" Solly and I said together.

"Kaspar himself told me during the job interview."

"Kaspar?" said Dad.

Principal Bentham went on, "He has a teaching certificate and proper qualifications, which he earned before committing his evil acts. His mother insisted on his having a profession to fall back on. And he took several refresher courses while in jail. You see, Manfred, Daisy, I believe that people deserve a chance to better themselves. Kaspar paid his debt to society. He is sorry for the bad things that he did – and let's admit it, they were whoppers. I mean, have you actually watched that old television show of his, *The Zoomers*? Making that was a crime in itself. But our justice system is not just about punishment. It is also about reform. So I am giving him this chance."

"He can't be trusted," Mom said. "He has fooled people before. He fooled us."

"Yes, I know. For that very reason, I am keeping a close eye on him. One sign of evil behavior and he will be dismissed immediately. And now, if you have any other concerns, my door is always welcome. Daisy, Manfred, it's good to see you, as always. But if I might ask, Manfred, why are you wearing your bathrobe?"

There wasn't anything for us to do, Dad said, but wait until Kaspar Snit showed his real motives for this bizarre behavior. So Mom and Dad let me go to class, but told me to be on the lookout. I went up to my classroom and hesitated at the door before knocking lightly and going in.

"Ah, Ms. Blande," Kaspar Snit said. "You are late."

"Here's my late slip, Mr. Sni – I mean, Mr. Parsstinka."

He looked at me hard and took the slip. "All right. Sit down. We were just discussing nuclear fusion."

I went to my desk and saw Fox, who gave me a funny look to try and make me laugh. I covered my mouth with my hand as I sat down. Then he leaned over and whispered, "You missed all the talk before class."

"What talk?" I whispered back.

"Some of the guys are going to try and get Parsstinka to blow his top."

"I don't think that's a very good idea."

"Ms. Blande," Kaspar Snit said sharply, "do you have something to share with the class?"

"Ah, no, sir, I was just borrowing a potato. I mean, a pencil."

"I don't think that requires lengthy discussion. Now, to continue. . . ."

The boy on my other side raised his hand.

"Yes, Mr. Tufts?" Kaspar Snit said.

"I have to go to the bathroom."

"Didn't you go just ten minutes ago?"

"Yeah, but now I need to take a bath."

The class broke up with laughter. Kaspar Snit smiled painfully. But all he said was "Very amusing. Now if we can get back to our discussion."

"Mr. Parsstinka?"

"Yes, Ms. Nubell?"

"Tomorrow is Crazy Hat Day. But the tradition in the school is that the teacher wears his crazy hat on the day before Crazy Hat Day."

"That sounds a bit odd. Are you sure?"

"Absolutely. And we think it would show real school spirit if you wore one."

"I'm sure it would. But, unfortunately, I did not know about this tradition and so I have no crazy hat."

"We could make one for you."

"Make one?"

"Sure," she said. "All we need is a piece of that foolscap on your desk."

"Well, I don't know."

"But it's the Inkpotts tradition," said Julia Worthington, from the back.

Kaspar Snit sighed. "All right, all right. I wouldn't like to break your precious tradition. But make it quickly, will you? We have a lot of work to cover."

Nora Nubell and Allen Tufts sprang up from their seats and went over to the teacher's desk. They took a sheet of foolscap, rolled it into a cone, and stuck on a piece of tape. "There you go," Nora said. "Put it on, Mr. Parsstinka."

Kaspar Snit looked dubiously at the foolscap that Nora had put into his hands. But he raised it up and put it on his head. Standing there in his black cape, with the paper cone on his head, he looked so ridiculous that I couldn't help giggling.

"And we have one more tradition," a boy named Ralph called out from the back.

"And what could that possibly be?" Kaspar Snit asked.

"We try to knock off the teacher's hat. Ready, everybody? One . . . two . . . *three!*"

Objects flew through the air – erasers, rubber balls, candies – towards Kaspar Snit. He held up his hands to protect himself, but he was pelted all over. Just as the hat was being knocked from his head, a camera flash went off. I turned to see Julia Worthington, standing up with the camera in her hand.

"That will be a great picture for the yearbook!" she said.

I looked at Kaspar Snit, waiting for him to explode. Waiting for him to do something terrible. But, instead, he just stood against the blackboard, eyes narrow, face boiling red, teeth bared. Finally he bent over, picked up the foolscap, put it on the desk, and said, "That's enough fun for one day, children. It's time to get to work."

Kaspar Snit didn't lose his temper, didn't punish us, didn't even raise his voice. After that, the kids were no longer afraid of him. They left their cell phones on to ring; somebody had a pizza delivered to the class; everybody dropped their pencils to make a loud clatter. Even the new boy, Fox, got in on it. I wanted to tell him not to, that Kaspar Snit was sure to take his vengeance on the class eventually. I even wanted to tell Fox about flying. I hadn't wanted to tell anyone about it before, and wanting to tell Fox felt really weird. But, of course, I didn't. I couldn't.

And so the only one who didn't misbehave was me, which made Allen Tufts call me a teacher's pet.

At one point, the class got so out of control that Principal Bentham came in and gave us a lecture about taking advantage of an inexperienced teacher. But still the class took advantage of him. And did Kaspar Snit finally blow his top? Did he yell and scream? Did he whip a stick of chalk at Allen Tufts's head, or pick up Nora Nubell by the collar?

No, he didn't. He didn't do anything except to ask, in a low and miserable voice, "Would everybody *please* be quiet."

What in the world was going on?

SUCH
EXCELLENT
COMPANY

On Saturday morning, as soon as I woke up, I remembered that we were going to Kaspar Snit's house for dinner. I went down the hall to see Solly in the living room, folding up the green pajama top he used as part of his Googoo-man costume. He put it into a cardboard box that already held the bottoms, the red bathing suit, the belt and towel-cape and goggles, and even the shoes with retractable roller skates.

"What are you doing?" I said.

"I'm putting Googoo-man into retirement. I'm sending my costume to the Superhero Hall of Fame in Kansas. They can put it on display with the other failures: Zipperman, Bouncy-boy, Puddle-woman."

"Solly, I really think that's a bad idea."

"Why?"

"Because we might need Googoo-man."

"You mean as a clown? So people can laugh at a kid wearing pajamas that are too small for him? Thanks anyway, Eleanor."

He closed the lid of the box and taped it closed. With a pen, he began to write out the address of the hall of fame. Shaking my head, I walked past him into the kitchen, where I found my dad reading the newspaper, in his bathrobe and needing a shave, as always.

Out loud, I said, *"Arrghh."*

Dad looked over the newspaper at me. "Did you just growl?"

"If I don't do something, I'm going to go crazy," I said. "Where are my rubber boots?"

"In the front closet. Why?"

"Because I, Eleanor Blande, lowly daughter of the world's foremost expert on fountains, declare this to be the long-overdue Fountain-Cleaning Day."

"I don't really feel like it," Dad said. "Maybe next weekend." He began reading his newspaper again.

"Fine. I'll clean it myself."

I marched out of the kitchen to the front closet, where I put on my boots, raincoat, and even a rain hat. I went back into the kitchen to find a bucket, a bottle of dishwashing soap, and a sponge under the sink. When I got up again, I saw that Solly and Mom had joined Dad and all of them were staring at me openmouthed. But I ignored them, walking between Mom and Dad to the front door and going outside.

"Okay, you win," I heard my dad call. "We're coming."

But I didn't care if they were coming. I opened the little door in the base of the statue and turned off the water to let it drain. Then I squirted soap into the bucket, poured in water with the hose by the side of the house, and got to work scrubbing the lower hooves of one of the horses. And I learned something pretty quickly: It's a lot easier to clean something regularly than to wait so long. It took a lot more muscle than usual to get off all that algae and dirt and bird poop.

In a few minutes, Mom, Dad, and Solly were working beside me, wielding their own mops and brushes, buckets and sponges. I guess Solly didn't find the work too hard because he started to sing.

Scrub, scrub, scrub that fountain,
The work is really nuttin'.
I'll start at the head, you start at the feet,
And we'll meet at the belly button!

A small crowd gathered to watch us, but we were used to that.

"Dad," I said, "I'm not sure it's a good idea to go to Kaspar Snit's dinner party tonight."

"Yeah," Solly said, wiping a blob of foam from his

nose. "I bet he's going to try and poison us. And I happen to be allergic to poison. Let's stay home and order pizza."

"That wouldn't be very polite," Dad said, from the top of a ladder. "Besides, right now we can't afford to order pizza. In fact, there are going to be no trips to the ice-cream parlor or any other treats for a while."

"Manfred," Mom said, "you don't have to tell them right now."

"They might as well know, Daisy. I might even have to sell some things."

"What sort of things?" I asked. But Dad didn't answer. I scrubbed the last bit of algae off a horse's tail and was just turning to get my bucket when I saw Kaspar Snit moving to the front of the crowd.

"Mr. Parsstinka," I said. My parents and Solly stopped what they were doing and turned too.

"So this is your famous fountain," Kaspar Snit said. "I've heard rather a lot about it."

"Did you know that someone almost ground it into aquarium gravel?" Solly said, narrowing his eyes.

"That would have been a terrible shame. I think the science of fountains might be quite interesting for my students. Perhaps Mr. Blande could come in and speak one day."

"Of course, if you'd like," Dad said.

"Excellent. I'm just on my way to the market to buy some fresh produce. After all, I'm making dinner tonight!

Good day to you all." Kaspar Snit touched the brim of his hat and slipped back into the crowd.

Mom insisted that we take showers and put on nice clothes before going to Kaspar Snit's house.

"Why do I have to look good when I'm just going to be trapped inside a giant drum, or strapped to a cannonball and shot into the stratosphere?" Solly said.

"You're not going to be shot anywhere," Mom said, standing at the bathroom door to make sure he was really combing his hair. "I'm sure it'll be a perfectly nice evening."

But Mom wasn't really so sure. When I went into the kitchen, I found a note left on the table. Mom must have slipped it there while we were getting ready.

To whom it may concern,

We have gone for dinner to the teacher Mr. Parsstinka's house. We will be home by nine o'clock. If we are not home by then, please call the policeman at the station who likes to tell jokes and let him know that we have been captured by Kaspar Snit.

Thank you for your assistance in this matter.

Daisy Galinski

I heard Dad calling for me and quickly put down the note, joining them all at the front door. Mom led the way down the front walk, carrying one of those boxes of fancy chocolates that you would never buy for yourself. Solly really had packed up his Googoo-man outfit. He wore a pair of stiff new trousers and a button-down shirt. He looked like a miniature accountant.

Ginger Hirshbein's old house was so close that it took us about forty-two seconds to get there. From the outside, the house didn't look any different, except that the flowers in the pots were dead and the curtains were closed and crabgrass had taken over the lawn and the porch was littered with flyers. Mom didn't slow down, but marched right up the steps to the front door. The rest of us had to follow.

Dad took a deep breath and rang the bell.

"Nobody's home," Solly said. "Let's go!" He was already turning around when the door opened.

There stood Kaspar Snit, wearing a chef's hat and an apron spattered with tomato sauce. He was holding a pot in one hand and a dripping spoon in the other.

"Come in, come in! I'm having a little kitchen emergency . . . nothing to get alarmed about, but if someone would be so kind as to grab the fire extinguisher. . . ."

Flames were shooting up from a saucepan on the stove. Dad took the extinguisher off a shelf and sprayed the flames to smother them. The smoke detector beeped so loudly that I had to cover my ears. Mom reached up, took the smoke detector off the wall, and pressed a button to make it stop. I noticed a book, open on the counter: *The Complete Nincompoop's Guide to Dinner Parties*. Maybe

Kaspar Snit hadn't read the part about not lighting the food on fire.

"Thank you," Kaspar Snit said, with visible relief, bending over to peer into the oven. "I had no idea that cheese was inflammable. Well, Eleanor, another lesson in the science of combustion. We shall have one less dish for dinner, but there's no cause for worry. We have plenty of food. Everything is just about ready. Why don't we all sit down?"

The dining-room table was a wooden door propped up by unpacked boxes at each end and surrounded by plastic lawn chairs. Kaspar Snit said, "You must excuse the setting for our dinner. I am not yet quite settled in. I had planned to buy more furniture, but I have been rather swamped with preparing classes and marking science reports. By the way, Eleanor, while a *B+* is a respectable mark on your own paper, I believe you can do better."

Just what I needed – a dinner party where my teacher told my parents I wasn't working hard enough.

Kaspar Snit turned to my father and said, "Is it all right if I call you Manfred?"

"Well, there's no point in calling him Steve," Solly answered.

"Yes, of course it's fine," Dad said.

"Perhaps, Manfred, you would open the wine while I serve?"

"It would be a pleasure," Dad said. The only problem was, Kaspar Snit didn't have a corkscrew. Dad had to pry the cork out with a screwdriver.

Meanwhile, Kaspar Snit began to serve the meal. "I know how fond you all are of Italian cuisine," he said, dishing out helpings of what looked like pasta soup. "I must have done something wrong," he said. "It's supposed to be lasagna."

"It looks perfect," Mom said. "Well, almost perfect."

Next came some sort of potato dish that I figured was supposed to be mashed, only it had come out rock hard. Then some shriveled green beans that looked like they'd been excavated from a prehistoric site.

After we were all served, and Solly and I had something called snellberry juice in our glasses and the adults had wine, Kaspar Snit sat down. A moment later, he jumped up and ran into the kitchen, this time coming back without the chef's hat and apron.

"Well," Dad said, "this is a true feast."

"Let us make a toast." Kaspar Snit held up his glass. "To . . . to Pittsburgh."

"Pittsburgh?" Mom asked.

"It just came into my head. I'm afraid that I'm very new at this. Everything seems so complicated. But please eat."

I saw my dad look doubtfully at his plate. He picked up his fork and scooped up some dripping lasagna. He closed his eyes, opened his mouth, and slipped in the fork. I watched him chew, half-expecting him to turn green or begin howling like a wolf. Instead, he opened his eyes and nodded. "Not bad," he pronounced. "It could use a touch more oregano."

"I tend to be conservative with my spices. After all, you can always add, but you can't take away."

Solly and I looked at each other, picked up our forks, and dug in. "*Hmm*, not bad," Solly said. "Kind of like a tomato milkshake. Do you have a straw?"

"I'm afraid not," Kaspar Snit said. He glanced quickly at the palm of his hand and said, "We are having very pleasant weather these days."

"Yes," Mom said. "Very pleasant."

Kaspar Snit glanced at his hand again. "Manfred, how is your fountain work proceeding?"

"What work? I don't have any at all."

"I'm so glad to hear it. And, Eleanor, have you had any enjoyable flying trips lately?"

"Not since that creature catcher, Levon du Plessy-Minsk, has been after me."

"Very nice, I'm sure."

"Why do you keep looking at your hand?" Solly said. "Hey, you've got writing there. Cheat notes!"

"All right, you caught me," Kaspar Snit said. "It's just a few lines. I find it so hard to make regular conversation."

"You're doing very well," Mom said.

Solly lifted his plate and tipped it into his mouth, slurping up lasagna juice.

"Where are your manners, Solly?" Mom said.

"What? It's a compliment to the chef."

"Such an angelic boy," Kaspar Snit said, with an uncomfortable smile.

"I am?"

"Perhaps I overstate the case. It's hard to get these things right. I believe it is time for dessert. Oh, dear."

"What is it?" Dad said.

"I forgot to make dessert."

Mom said, "The chocolates that we brought will do just fine. You worked very hard, Kaspar, and we appreciate it. Why don't we sit in the living room?"

"Yes, very good," Kaspar Snit said, looking relieved not to have to make a decision. The only problem was, when we got to the living room, there were no chairs to sit on. Or sofa. There was only a cardboard box marked SOCKS (BLACK), UNDERWEAR (BLACK), UNDERSHIRTS (BLACK).

"Not to worry," Dad said quickly. "This family enjoys standing, don't we? Daisy, how about those chocolates?"

Kaspar Snit took a chocolate from the box that my mother was holding out to him and began to chew it, without pleasure.

Finally, Mom said, "Kaspar, I think you better tell us what exactly is going on."

Kaspar Snit looked down at the ground and scuffed one pointed black shoe against the other. "You're right. I can no longer keep it a secret."

"This ought to be good," Solly said.

"I am trying to give up being an evil genius."

"You're kidding," Dad said.

"Alas, no."

"Maybe you're trying to trick us again," I said.

"If it were only so. That would be so much easier, so much more natural for me."

"But why would you give up being an evil genius when you're so good at it?" Solly asked.

"Because something happened to me in jail. You see, I used to lie on my bed at night and look up at the ceiling. Actually, I used to look at the bottom of the bunk above me, where Bernard slept. Car thief. Excellent chess player."

"You're getting a bit off topic," Dad said.

"Yes, of course. When I used to lie in bed, an image came to me every night. A haunting image. I tried to shake it off, to get it out of my head, but it always returned. Hovering over me. Speaking to me."

"What was it?" Mom asked.

"It was . . . it was *Lucretia Leer!*"

"Mrs. Leer?" I said.

"Yes, the very one – the nanny who took care of you. It was her face scowling at me, talking to me. No matter what I did, I could not get her to go away."

"What was she saying?" Mom asked.

"Those words are seared in my brain. *'You are a cad. Yes, a cad, a scallywag, and a nogoodnik.'* Such sweet words! Such music to my ears!"

"Sweet?" Solly said. "Music?"

"Yes, indeed. For, you see – oh, this is so very hard for someone like me to say – for you see, I had fallen *in love*."

"Oh, my goodness!" said Mom.

"Gross," said Solly.

Kaspar Snit shook his head despairingly. "I thought the same thing. I tried to free myself of the feeling. I worked at having evil thoughts. I tried to come up with terrifically

66

awful schemes. But nothing worked. I was hooked. I'm *still* hooked. And there doesn't seem to be anything that I can do about it. I am in love with Lucretia Leer."

"But, Kaspar," Mom said, "being in love isn't a bad thing. It's a good thing."

"Of course it is," Dad said, coming forward. He was about to put his hand on Kaspar Snit's shoulder, but thought better of it. "And I suppose it explains why you've became a teacher."

Kaspar Snit nodded solemnly. "I have to do something other than stealing, swindling, lying, coercing, and bullying – all the good old ways. I need a regular life. When I was a young man, my mother insisted that I get a teaching certificate, like she had. Even an evil genius wants to please his mother sometimes."

"But why teach here?" I asked. "I mean, why our school? And why our street?"

"I thought that you and your family would be a good influence. And, to be honest, although I could hardly call you friends, you're the only people I know. Except for my old assistant."

"You mean Slouch?" I asked.

"Yes, Slouch. And he was even less of a friend than all of you. In fact, I despised Slouch. He was immature, annoying, mean, lazy, insincere, and totally selfish. Of course, that made him perfect for the job, but he certainly wouldn't be friendship material."

Mom said, "Well, I just think your falling in love with Mrs. Leer is the most romantic thing I've ever heard."

Solly said, "I think it's the most nauseating thing I've ever heard."

"I am afraid it is a romance doomed to failure," Kaspar Snit said. "After all, I did hold her captive in Misery Mountain."

"Not to mention feeding us oatmeal with asparagus and mushroom-raisin sauce," Solly added.

"All too true," Kaspar Snit said. "And, of course, there is perhaps the biggest impediment of all – the memory of the dear, dreary Mr. Leer. I could never be a replacement for that towering figure of a man."

"I have to admit," Dad said, "that you're in a bit of a tough spot. Winning over Mrs. Leer is not going to be easy."

"But nothing is hopeless," I said. "I mean, you can try, can't you? And the worst that happens is, you get your heart stomped on."

"I'm not sure I'd put it that way," Mom said, "but Eleanor is right."

"I do want to try," said Kaspar Snit, wringing his long fingers. "But there is yet a last and most formidable obstacle in my path – my own evil genius. The pull is very strong. All of my ideas until now have been nasty ones. It is a hard habit to break."

"An interesting challenge," Dad said, rubbing his chin. "How do you take the 'evil' out of 'evil genius'?"

We stood in the empty living room, all of us thinking about Kaspar Snit's enormous challenge. Solly reached out his hand and plucked another chocolate from the box in Mom's hand. He popped it into his mouth.

"Cherry ripple," he mumbled.

And then, suddenly, I had it. "I know," I said. "It's simple."

Everybody turned to look at me. "Solly and I can help you to be a regular, decent human being," I explained. "We can teach you. It'll take a lot of work, especially as Mrs. Leer is coming to visit in just two weeks, but I think we can do it."

"Two weeks!" Kaspar Snit groaned. "I can't possibly have the evil squeezed out of me in just two weeks."

"Sure you can," Solly said, a slow grin breaking on his face. "If *we* do the squeezing."

"That's right," I said. "We'll transform you."

"We'll reconstruct you," Solly added.

"We'll refashion you."

"We'll improve you."

"We'll take you apart and put you back together."

"That's enough, you two," Mom said. "Kaspar gets the picture. I think it's an excellent idea. It won't be easy, but it's just possible. And you don't have to become a saint, Kaspar. Eleanor and Solly can teach the teacher."

Kaspar Snit sighed. "All right," he said. "I agree to it. Really, I have no choice." He looked straight at me. "But don't think I'm going to enjoy it. . . ."

THE
FIRST
LESSON

As if I could possibly get to sleep that night! *Kaspar Snit wants to give up being an evil genius? He's in love with Mrs. Leer?* It was just too weird.

Solly probably couldn't sleep either. No doubt he was lying there, thinking how strange it was too. I decided to creep into his room so that at least we could talk about it. Pulling aside the covers, I got my flashlight from the night table drawer and turned on its beam of light. Quickly I opened my own door and closed it again, then slid along the wall to Solly's, like a jewel thief in an old movie. Opening his door, I slipped inside and gently closed it.

"Solly?" I whispered.

Nothing.

"Solly?" I said, a little louder.

"Ah . . . *ooommm.*"

"You're awake too, right?"

"Sorry . . . I'm . . . retired . . . superhero . . ."

I pointed the flashlight towards Solly's bed. He was half off, legs in the air, facedown on the floor carpet. I couldn't count on him for anything.

"Thanks a lot," I whispered.

"Shmoogassy," he mumbled back.

Closing the door behind me, I turned off the flashlight. I didn't want to go back to bed, so I slid along the hallway to the living room.

Where I found my mom again, standing at the open window.

She didn't look as if she was trying to fly, but was staring outside like she had given up. I hesitated, but finally decided to approach her.

"Beautiful night, isn't it?" she said.

"I guess so. What are you thinking about, Mom?"

"The very first time that I ever flew . . ."

"When you were just a little older than me, right?"

"That's right. It was a night like this – lots of stars, the air carrying the scent of spring. Everybody else was asleep. I was afraid and excited at the same time. I closed my eyes and put my hands at my sides, like I'd seen my own mother do. I cleared my mind. And then, a moment later, I felt the air touching my skin. I flew all night and when I finally came home, the dawn was just breaking. I was so tired. But I thought I'd found the one thing that I needed, the one thing that would always make me happy."

"And now you don't have it," I said.

"Yes. But I was wrong about the one thing. It wasn't the only thing I needed to make me happy. I need you and Solly. And your father. And I still have all of you, so it's all right."

"But you need something for yourself, too, Mom. You need to get over being afraid."

"Anyway, enough about me. What's going on with you? Couldn't sleep?"

"I don't know," I said. "It's just hard to think of Kaspar Snit as anything but bad. I mean, it's hard to imagine a person in a new way."

"I know. We get an idea about someone and it's hard to change. I remember when I met your father, I thought he was awful."

"Really?"

"Uh-huh. I thought he was arrogant and stuck-up. He wouldn't talk to anybody. But then I realized he wasn't arrogant, he was just shy. If I hadn't got past my first impression . . . well, you wouldn't be here."

"But the way I think about Kaspar Snit isn't just a first impression," I said.

"That's true. On the other hand, you've always believed that there was something else inside him, Eleanor, something better. And you were right. If he's capable of having feelings for Mrs. Leer, then maybe he's capable of a lot more. But enough about him. What about you? Solly tells me there's a new boy in your class."

"Remind me to murder Solly."

"Does this new boy have a name?"

"No."

"Is he cute?"

"Can we not talk about this?"

"Sure, sweetie. Did you want to go for a little fly?"

"No, that's okay."

"You're afraid it'll be hard for me to watch. Don't worry. I'll wait for you and you can tell me about it when you get back. That might help."

"Okay. Thanks."

Mom stepped away to give me the space in front of the open window. I closed my eyes, adjusted my hands and feet, and a moment later I was hovering over our house. I flew over our sleeping town, looking down at the buildings and parks, the squares and shops. Above the Constance Foote Museum of Art, I could see a banner between the columns and I swooped low enough to read the words: OPENING SOON! ANCIENT SPLENDOR: GOLD, SILVER, JEWELRY, AND OTHER VALUABLE STUFF FROM THE STATE TREASURES OF VERULIA. I thought of His Excellency H. Waldorf Mansfield, the ambassador of Verulia, and wondered if he was inside, sleeping with his country's precious treasures.

Circling around, I headed home. As I approached our neighborhood, I kept a lookout for Levon du Plessy-Minsk's minivan, but I didn't see it. I got closer to our house and started to descend, until I was just above the treetops. I could see the dark shapes of lawn furniture, teeter-totters, and barbecues in the backyards.

And then I saw the dark figure of a man, standing on a front lawn. A tremble of fear ran through me when I saw that the figure was looking up at me. *Was it that awful creature catcher?*

No, it wasn't him. It was Kaspar Snit, carrying his garbage can. He slowly raised one hand and waved at me as I flew past.

Solly and I didn't just march over to Kaspar Snit's house after school on Monday and start transforming him into a decent member of society. We needed to prepare. In just two weeks, Mrs. Leer was coming to visit us, and that wasn't a long time to convert an evil genius. The truth was, I wasn't even sure it was possible. But we had to give it our best shot.

So Solly and I spent Sunday getting ready to be his teachers. We went into my room and I stuck a big sheet of paper on the back of the door. "Okay," I said to Solly, "we need to come up with a lesson plan. A plan that's going to turn Kaspar Snit into a regular person. Like Mom said to us, he doesn't have to be a saint. Or good or nice every moment. But he can't be kidnapping people, or taking pleasure in making kids miserable. The question is, what will our lessons be?"

Solly sat on my desk chair and put his hands on his head, like he was concentrating. Suddenly he grinned. "I've got one," he said.

By the end of the day – with breaks for snacks and lunch, of course – we had them all. Ten lessons that we hoped would do the trick. They weren't exactly your usual sort of lessons, but then, this wasn't like teaching somebody fractions or how to swim. When we were done, we presented the list to our parents, neatly written out on the big sheet.

Mom and Dad were sitting on the living-room sofa. They read the lessons from top to bottom and read them again.

"They're . . . interesting," Dad said, looking at Mom.

"You've definitely put a lot of thought into them," Mom said, looking at Dad.

"But do you think they'll work?" I asked.

"About number two," Dad said. "Do you think that's necessary?"

"Crucial," Solly answered, crossing his arms. "I came up with that one."

"I'm not quite sure about number seven," Mom said. "And how are you even going to get –"

"I've already got that figured out," I said.

Dad rubbed his chin. "Well, I don't have any better ideas. I say, go for it."

"We're rooting for you," Mom added.

I smiled. "School," I said, "is about to begin."

Solly nodded. "This is going to be better than my birthday."

In class on Monday morning, Kaspar Snit hardly looked at me. When I put up my hand, he didn't pick me, and even when I talked to Fox, he didn't tell me to pipe down.

Maybe he was having second thoughts about making Solly and me his teachers. I couldn't blame him – I had a few second thoughts myself.

When the last bell of the day went, I raced outside and waited for Solly. For once he wasn't late and the two of us ran home together. We carefully removed the big sheet on the wall, rolled it up, grabbed the box we needed, and went out the front door again. In a minute, we were at Kaspar Snit's house. His bicycle was by the door, so we knew he was home from school.

"Ready?" I asked Solly.

He took a deep breath. "Ready as I'll ever be."

I knocked on the door. Almost instantly, it opened. There stood Kaspar Snit.

"You are here," he said.

"Yes," I answered solemnly.

"You have come to instruct me."

"Yes," I said again.

Kaspar Snit swallowed hard. "I shall be a willing pupil," he said.

"Great," Solly said. "Now this is the part where you let us into the house."

"Oh, right."

Kaspar Snit moved aside to let us in. "Shall we sit down?" he said. But there were still no chairs in the living room.

"That's all right," I answered. "We have a lesson plan for you. If you don't mind, we'd like to put it up on the wall."

"A lesson plan? Yes, certainly. I am anxious to see it."

Solly and I taped the plan to the wall. We stepped back and watched as Kaspar Snit began to read.

TEN LESSONS FOR KASPAR SNIT

Lesson one:	*Play a game of Monopoly*
Lesson two:	*Build a rowboat*
Lesson three:	*Tell a joke*
Lesson four:	*Learn to dance*
Lesson five:	*Write a poem*
Lesson six:	*Get a pet*
Lesson seven:	*Take care of a baby*
Lesson eight:	*Perform a heroic act*
Lesson nine:	*Sacrifice yourself for your friends*
Lesson ten:	*Do something surprising*

Kaspar Snit must have finished reading, but he kept staring at the sheet. His mouth curled down into a dark pout. Finally, he said, "Is this some kind of a joke?"

"No joke," I answered. "It's for real."

"These lessons are ridiculous. *Build a rowboat. Take care of a baby. Sacrifice myself for my friends.* I don't have any friends! You're not trying to teach me anything; you're trying to make me look like a fool."

"No, honest we're not. We're trying to help you. Solly and I have thought about these lessons a lot. You're just going to have to trust us."

"You can trust us, can't you?" Solly said, batting his eyelashes.

"I don't know. . . ."

"Listen, sis," Solly said, turning to me. "We've got other clients. If Mr. Snit here isn't ready for our ten-step program, we'll spend our time with someone who is. Come on."

"You're right," I said. "Let's go."

We both stepped towards the sheet and started to take it down. But Kaspar Snit said, "No, leave it. I trust you. I really have no choice but to put my fate in your hands. Where do we begin?"

"With lesson one, naturally," I said. "Besides, it's the easiest. All you have to do is play Monopoly with me and Solly. We've even brought our game."

"That will be easy enough," Kaspar Snit said, with a glint in his eye. He rubbed his hands together as Solly laid the board out on the carpet. "I shall demolish the both of you. No one has ever defeated me in Monopoly."

"You do have a lot to learn," I said, putting out the Monopoly money. Solly and I sat cross-legged on the carpet. Kaspar Snit looked at us and then lowered himself, groaning.

"I shall be the hat," Kaspar Snit said, scooping up the little silver piece.

"But I'm always the hat," Solly whined. "It's my favorite. Aren't I always the hat, Eleanor?"

"Sure. When we play, you are."

"Well, you're not just playing with your sister, are you? So pick something else, crybaby."

"*Ahem*," I cleared my throat. "Kaspar, perhaps you might remember who is the adult here and who is the kid."

"That means I should give in to every bratty request? Fine. You can have the stupid hat. I'll take the car. All the better to run you over with, ha!"

This was not a good start. I chose the dog and we started to play. I was never much for games, mostly because I didn't really care if I won or not, but Solly loved to compete. He and Kaspar Snit raced to buy properties, houses, and hotels. When Kaspar Snit landed on Solly's Kentucky Avenue, Solly pumped his fist and shouted, "Oh, yeah, oh, yeah!" And when Solly landed on Kaspar Snit's Oriental Avenue, which had two houses, Kaspar Snit cackled with delight. And when I ended up with a GO DIRECTLY TO JAIL; DO NOT PASS GO card, they both snickered at me. I hardly knew who was worse.

After forty minutes, I was losing badly. Both of my opponents were sucking me dry and, a few minutes later, I was bankrupt.

"Okay, Snit," Solly said, rubbing his hands in imitation of an evil genius. "Now that the amateur is out of the way, you're going to see a true professional at work. Prepare yourself for defeat."

"Do you think so?" Kaspar Snit said evenly. "Or will you soon be running home to your mommy?"

This was getting ugly. The game went on. Kaspar Snit and Solly were pretty evenly matched, but after another half hour or so, Kaspar managed to buy Park Place, which gave him the three most valuable properties on the board. He put up three houses and Solly immediately landed on one. "Now who's the professional?" Kaspar said, snapping his fingers. "Oh, I'm good. I am *so* good."

A couple of minutes later, while Solly was reading a Community Chest card, I whispered in Kaspar Snit's ear. "Solly's been feeling kind of down lately. It would be nice if you let him win."

"What?" Kaspar exclaimed, leaning away from me. "And look like a loser? Why, I'd rather –"

"Remember," I said quietly, "this is lesson number one. You've got a bigger goal here than winning a board game."

"Fine, fine," he said sulkily. Then he picked up the dice, threw them, and moved his piece. "Well, well," he said. "I don't believe anyone owns Virginia Avenue. I'll just –" I nudged Kaspar Snit with my elbow. "On the other hand, perhaps I'll pass on it," he said mournfully. "It's your turn, Solly."

"What a bad decision!" Solly said, with glee. "You could have blocked me from putting up houses. Now I'm going to crush you." Which is just what Solly proceeded to do.

Kaspar Snit did nothing to stop him. His money disappeared and his real-estate empire crumbled.

"That is the last of my properties," Kaspar Snit said. "I am bankrupt."

"I've won, I've won!" Solly did a victory dance, hooting and cheering. He sang out, "I beat Kaspar Snit, I beat Kaspar Snit. . . ."

Standing up, Kaspar leaned over to me. "Just look at him gloat," he said. "I could have won easily. Was that really the easy lesson?"

"By far," I said.

"Well, it is enough for today. I feel quite ill. If you would be so kind as to leave me in peace, I shall go and lie down with a bag of ice on my head."

"We've got to get home for dinner anyway," I said. "See you tomorrow."

"Don't be a sore loser!" Solly called, as we went out the door. Halfway across the street, I looked back to see Kaspar Snit, standing in his doorway, looking at us and rubbing the fingers of one hand against his forehead.

THIS CHAPTER CONTAINS BAD WORDS

I didn't think that Kaspar Snit's first lesson had gone that well, even if he did let Solly win. After all, attitude was the most important thing and his really stunk. But when I told Mom about it, she said that we shouldn't get discouraged. It was hard for people to change – for smokers to stop smoking, for junk-food eaters to begin eating healthy food – but that they could if they wanted to enough. And Kaspar Snit, she said, was *motivated*.

For Kaspar Snit's second lesson, he had to build a rowboat. This might seem like a strange task, but Solly and I felt pretty sure about it, even though we, ourselves, had no idea how to build one. "I've never even made a bird-house," Kaspar Snit said, but we didn't give in. It was a good thing that the lesson came after school on Friday, because it took Kaspar Snit the whole weekend. He bought a book on woodworking, then went to the lumberyard and bought planks, nails, saws, and hammers. Then he got to work in his backyard. Whenever we dropped in to see how he was doing, he complained to us bitterly, holding up his fingers. They were covered in Band-Aids from all the times he had hit them with the hammer.

Late on Sunday afternoon, Kaspar Snit rang our doorbell. He was covered in sawdust, his face streaked with dirt, but he was holding a crude-looking paddle and had a gleam of triumph in his eye.

"You didn't think I could do it, did you? Well, come and take a look!" Kaspar Snit led the way to his house, holding the paddle up like a flag. Mom and Dad came too. There in Kaspar Snit's backyard was a rowboat. Okay, it wasn't exactly perfect. The sides were crooked, one of the boards had been repaired with three crosspieces of wood, but it was a rowboat all right. And he had made it with his own hands. It even had a name painted on the bow: *Lucretia*.

Solly and I looked at each other. "Pretty cool," Solly said.

"It is really very satisfying to make something with my very own hands," Kaspar Snit said. "I would never have believed it. Several times, people came around to watch me. I had to talk to them like I was, well, normal. It was quite an experience."

"That's terrific," Mom said.

"I wonder," Dad said gently, "if it's seaworthy."

"I believe it is," Kaspar Snit said. "But there is only one way to prove it. We must put it in the water. But where?"

"There's a pond in the park," Mom said.

"Excellent! We must go and try it right away. I simply cannot wait."

Dad brought his car around and we all helped to lift the rowboat onto the roof rack. Dad tied it down and we piled into the car. Kaspar Snit sat in the middle of the backseat, with his knees sticking up. "I must admit," he said, "that was an excellent lesson. I should not have doubted you. I feel like I've really accomplished something."

Mom turned and gave us the thumbs-up. We got to the park and half-carried, half-dragged the rowboat down to the pond. Two swans squawked at us as they got out of the way.

"Can we go for a row too?" Solly said.

"Of course," Kaspar Snit said. "But if you do not mind, I would like to be the first." In a louder voice he said, "I christen thee *Lucretia*!" Then he pushed the rowboat off the shore, jumping into it as it floated out. It wobbled a little as Kaspar Snit sat down, but then it steadied. He began to row, first on one side and then on the other, and the boat moved towards the center of the pond.

"Isn't it marvelous?" Kaspar Snit cried. "'Sailing, sailing, over the ocean blue . . .'"

"How lovely," said Mom.

"Is it my imagination," said Dad, "or is the boat getting lower?"

It *was* getting lower. Kaspar Snit looked down into the boat. "What's this? I'm getting wet! There seems to be the tiniest of leaks. Wait, it's getting larger. . . ."

He cupped his hands and began to bail frantically, tossing handfuls of water over the side. But the boat filled up more and more, until Kaspar Snit was practically floating in it.

Then it sank.

Kaspar Snit sputtered as he flailed his arms. Then he began to swim. As he waded onto the shore, we rushed forward to help him out.

"All that work for nothing!" he cried, as water dripped from his mustache and his cape. "I'm no good at building, or anything else that regular people do!"

He stomped his feet, half in anger at us and half, I thought, at himself. But then he stopped and stood before us, a puddle forming around his feet. "Excuse me," he said, "I am making a spectacle of myself. I apologize. Perhaps being disappointed is a lesson too. Now if you don't mind, I would like to go home."

His shoes squeaked as he walked towards the car. In the backseat, I could feel how cold and wet he was. We let him off in front of his house and then we drove to ours.

"Nothing," Solly said, "is more pathetic than a soaking-wet evil genius."

"Former evil genius," I corrected him.

In school on Monday morning, Kaspar Snit still had a couple of Band-Aids on his fingers. This time he nodded to me when he came in and even said, "Good morning, Ms. Blande." Then he began his lesson, which he called a scientific explanation of the sinking of the *Titanic*.

Oh, brother.

Lesson three began right after school. For two solid hours, Solly and I taught Kaspar Snit how to tell a joke – the one that our uncle Seymour had told us when he came to visit from Yellowknife last year. The joke went like this:

Two little kids were lying in bed before falling asleep.

The first one said, "I think it's time we learned to use bad words."

The second one said, "Great. How do we do it?"

The first kid said, "Tomorrow I'm going to say the word 'hell' and you can use the word 'ass.'"

The second kid agreed and so they went to sleep.

In the morning, they couldn't wait to try out their words. They ran to the kitchen. Their mom asked, "What would you like for breakfast?"

The first kid said, "Aw, hell, I'll have some Cheerios."

When the mom heard that, she took away the first kid's television privileges for a week. Then she asked the second kid what he would like for breakfast.

"I don't know," said the second kid, "but you can bet your ass it isn't Cheerios."

When Uncle Seymour told it to me and Solly, we laughed pretty hard. You might think that learning to tell a joke would be a cinch, but it wasn't. For one thing, when we told it to Kaspar Snit, he didn't laugh. He thought that the mother had been too easy on the kid – that the punishment should have been worse. "Come on," Solly said, in exasperation. "It's a *joke*. Ha-ha? Funny?" So Kaspar Snit pretended to think it was funny and forced himself to laugh, which was an awful sound, like a chicken being strangled.

Still, we began to teach him the joke. Learning the words wasn't hard – it was the emphasis and the timing that were important. After those two hours, Kaspar Snit suddenly said, "Enough! I can't rehearse this stupid joke anymore. Give me the chance to tell it and you'll see. I'll have my audience rolling with laughter. They'll laugh until it hurts."

"I don't know," I said. "Your timing is still a bit weird."

"I've got my own comic style, that's all. Let's get this lesson over with."

"Hey," said Solly. "You think I *want* to spend my time this way? I could be reading comics, or mixing disgusting ingredients together in a bowl, or drawing all over my face. I'm making a sacrifice here."

"All right, all right," Kaspar Snit said. "But I know I'm ready. Give me a shot."

"Okay," I said. "Mom should be home from work now and Dad's making dinner. You can tell it to them."

"Fine. Just you see. I'm going to knock 'em dead."

The three of us slunk down the street to our house – "slunk" because Kaspar Snit was afraid that another student from Inkpotts Public School would see him and wonder what we were up to. As we entered the house, I called out, "Mom, Dad, Kaspar Snit has a joke for you!"

We found them in the kitchen, Mom laying out dishes and Dad hovering over a pot. "Having another lesson?" Dad said.

"Manfred, Daisy," said Kaspar Snit, clearing his throat. "If you would be so kind as to oblige me, I would like to tell you a humorous anecdote. I believe you will find it most amusing."

Mom put down a fork and turned to listen. "We're all ears," she said.

"Very good." Kaspar Snit clasped his hands in front of him as if he were going to sing in a choir. "Once upon a time there were two young men. Well, not men but boys actually, quite young, although I don't know their exact ages. Or their names. In any case, these two boys shared a room and one night in bed, when no doubt they were not supposed to be talking – and you know even better than me how children can be – one of the boys said to the other one, 'I believe the time has come for us to use socially unacceptable words.'"

"Kaspar –" I started.

"Please, Eleanor, do not interrupt. I am on a roll. The second child, no doubt highly influenced by the first, agreed to the idea. They settled on two words that I hope you shall not be overly offended by. If you are, I apologize in advance. The words are 'hell.' And 'ass.' I would have preferred to use 'heck' and 'bottom,' but my instructors assured me that the joke requires the original words. Well, these two young ruffians went to sleep, but in the morning, unfortunately, they remembered their plan.

"Down to the kitchen they went, where they encountered their mother. I do not know where the father was. Perhaps he had already left for work. Perhaps the mother was a single parent. This detail was not shared with me. The mother, no doubt wanting to ensure that her children had a good start to the day, asked the first boy what he would like for breakfast.

"'Oh, hell, I will have some healthful cereal,' the boy said. Naturally, the mother was appalled. She lectured the boy on the need for decent language and then forbade him television for a month. As well, he had to get an after-school job. Then she asked the second boy what he would like for his repast, hoping, of course, that his choice of breakfast food would also be of the sort that allows for the proper growth of body and mind.

"'I don't know,' said the second boy, who was probably younger than the first, although I don't have positive proof, 'but you can bet your ass' – again, I apologize for this apparently necessary word – 'that it won't be healthful cereal.'"

Kaspar Snit stopped talking. He stood, hands clasped, an expectant look on his face. Our parents did not speak for a good two minutes.

"That's it?" Dad said. "That's the end?"

"Quite so," Kaspar Snit said.

"Oh, oh, well, very funny," Mom said, trying to laugh.

"Yes, very droll," said Dad. "Very, very droll."

Kaspar Snit looked soundly defeated. He sighed deeply and looked down at his shoes.

"You see?" he said. "I knew it wasn't a very good joke."

We gave lesson four on Tuesday, but for this one we needed to ask my mother to come home early from work. The reason was, neither Solly nor I knew how to dance. At least, not the sort of dances – the waltz, the fox-trot, the rumba – that my parents always did at weddings, embarrassing us. Mrs. Leer had once told us that next to playing her pennywhistle, her greatest love was dancing. That was why we'd made it a lesson. The only problem was, Mom wasn't so keen on dancing with Kaspar Snit. But Dad encouraged her. "Don't think of him as the man who tried to put us into his marble-crushing machine," Dad said. "Think of him as a man in love." So Mom went.

And actually, it wasn't so bad. Kaspar Snit, with his long legs and gangly arms, turned out to be a pretty natural dancer. He picked up the steps quickly, and soon he and Mom were gliding across Kaspar Snit's smooth kitchen floor to the sound of an orchestra coming from a little radio.

"You're rather good at this," Mom said, just before Kaspar Snit dipped her. Kaspar smiled, and the sun glinted off his teeth.

A LITTLE CRIME

With four lessons done and six to go, Kaspar Snit wasn't doing too badly. The dancing went so well that we even thought he enjoyed becoming a regular person. But the very next morning, at breakfast, Dad opened the paper. "You two better listen to this," he said.

BIRTHDAY PARTY RAID LEAVES KIDS IN TEARS
Special to the Sentinel
Last evening was supposed to be the highlight of the year for little Orlando Rivington of 136 Sussex Drive. It was Orlando's sixth birthday, and he and his friends were having a party at the Pete's Pizza restaurant. But just as Mrs. Rivington was about to cut the cake for her son, a man swooped through the doors and scooped it up. Next he

popped all the balloons with a pin. He even twisted Mr. Rivington's nose before making his getaway. The unhappy children began to howl, but the cake was not recovered.

Later that evening, Officer Yogis of the local police station said, "It's a little crime, but a low and dastardly one. I look forward to catching the meany who did it."

A description of the culprit has been released. He is tall, wears a black cape, has a curling mustache, and giggles diabolically. Anyone seeing a person fitting this description should contact the police immediately.

Dad folded the newspaper and looked at Solly and me. "What do you think?" he asked. "Maybe our reformed evil genius isn't so reformed after all."

"But he's motivated," I said.

"It does sound like him," Mom admitted.

"Sure, it sounds like him," Solly said. "But do you know how many people out there wear capes and have curling mustaches? I mean, there must be dozens. Hundreds, even. . . ."

"I really think he wants to change," I said weakly.

"Maybe he does," Dad said. "It could be just a little slipup. You know, like someone trying to quit biting his nails who does it without thinking. After all, as evil deeds go, it wasn't exactly a biggie."

"We're supposed to give Kaspar Snit another lesson after school today," I said. What I didn't say, but what I thought was *maybe we should give up all together.*

"Do you think he's got any of the birthday cake left?" Solly asked hopefully.

"Solly!" Mom said. "You are not allowed to eat stolen birthday cake."

"Mom's right," Dad said. "It would make you an accessory to the crime."

"Even if it has pink frosting?" Solly said.

The bell was about to ring; Solly and I had to hustle to make it to school on time. I wanted to get to class before the other kids and so I shouted for Solly to hurry and started to run, my knapsack bouncing against my back. Usually he skated behind me on his retractable roller blades, but now that he had given up his Googoo-man outfit, Solly had to run like everybody else.

We made it to school three minutes before the bell. I hurried up the stairs to my homeroom. Kaspar Snit was taking papers out of his briefcase and putting them on his desk, along with a lunch bag with pictures from *Sesame Street*. "Ah," he said, as we came in. "My teachers and tormentors. Have you come to give me my next assignment?"

I crossed my arms and stared hard at him. Solly looked at me and did the same.

"What? What did I do?" Kaspar Snit said, like a little kid with chocolate smeared on his face.

"It's about a certain birthday party," I said.

"It's about not sharing cake with your instructors," Solly added.

"Is this some kind of riddle? Let me see. 'Party' rhymes with 'smarty.' And 'cake' rhymes with 'snake.' You want me to teach a snake to eat Smarties?"

Kaspar Snit was doing a pretty good job of acting innocent. I said, "You mean, you don't know about a kid's birthday party being raided yesterday by a man in a cape?"

"You balloon buster," Solly said.

"Cake, balloons? I don't know what you're talking about. I stayed home and watched reruns of *The Zoomers* on cable."

"Which episodes?" Solly said.

"I can't remember. All I remember is what a bad actor Slouch was. Such a ham! And he wasn't much better as an assistant."

"You're changing the subject," I said. "I'm just, well, very disappointed."

"Really, Eleanor," Kaspar Snit said. "Raiding a kiddy party? Does that sound like my style? All right, I used to like being mean to kids. But I'd be embarrassed to do something so insignificant. I have my pride, you know. Are you coming to the house for my next lesson or not?"

I looked at Kaspar Snit, who looked back at me. "Fine," I said. "And you better be ready."

"Yeah," Solly said, putting his hands on his hips. "And you better have some milk and cookies out too."

"Fine. Now if you would please start acting like I'm the teacher. The bell's about to ring."

Just then it did. Kids were galloping up the stairs and pouring into class. Solly said, "Thanks for the extra help,

Mr. Parsstinka," and hurried out. Julia came in and so did Fox, who walked beside me as we went to our desks.

"Hey, Eleanor," he said, "what's up?"

"Nothing much. You?"

"Nothing either."

He was so easy to talk to! We sat down. Kaspar Snit closed the door and rapped on the blackboard for our attention. "Listen up," he said. "We're going to be studying wave theory today and I want you to concentrate. Yes, this might seem like university-level material, but I'm sure if you put some effort into it . . . must we be interrupted?"

Someone had rapped loudly on the door. Kaspar Snit opened it and there stood Levon du Plessy-Minsk.

"Mr. Parsstinka, I am sorry to interrupt your class," he said. "But I've had a great breakthrough in finding the Mysterious Flying Girl."

"You have?"

"Yes, and tonight is very important."

"But what has this to do with my students?"

"I need to speak to my son. He's in your class."

Levon du Plessy-Minsk had a kid in our class? I started to look around when he called out, "Fox, please come here."

Fox? No! It couldn't be! It just couldn't! But there was Fox, getting up reluctantly and shuffling to the front of the room.

"Fox, I want you home right after school. We're going out in the minivan tonight."

"But, Dad, I've got soccer practise. Do I have to? And I was hoping to hang out with my friends. . . ."

"But this is vastly more important. This is about my career, my fame. Do you understand? I need your help getting ready. You'll just have to miss practise and your friends today."

"Oh, all right."

"Good boy. Now go back to your seat. Again, my apologies, Mr. Parsstinka."

"I should think so," Kaspar Snit muttered, as he closed the door. He began to draw an elaborate diagram on the board, but I couldn't have cared less. What a horror. *Fox du Plessy-Minsk!* My life was ruined.

For the rest of class, kids gave their science presentations. Kaspar Snit barely hid his boredom. He tossed pencils into a glass jar. He flossed his teeth. Finally he fell asleep, leaning back in his chair. When the bell went to end the period, he jerked awake and fell backwards, knocking his head on the blackboard.

For the rest of the day, I felt like a zombie. All I could think about was that Fox was the son of Levon du Plessy-Minsk, which meant that he was helping to catch the Mysterious Flying Girl, who was me. How would he feel if he knew? Would he think of me the same way that his dad thought of Bigfoot or the Loch Ness Monster?

By the time I met Solly after school, I was feeling pretty glum. "Hey, sis," he said. "Ready to give lesson number five? I wonder what kind of cookies Kaspar Snit will have for us. Double chocolate chip, maybe. Or those yummy ones with marshmallow inside."

"Solly," I said hesitantly. "What if you, you know, liked somebody, but were afraid the person might think you were a freak?"

"But you are a freak, so what's the problem?" he said. I swiped at his head, but he was prepared and ducked in time. "Okay, okay. Sorry. Do you mean, what if I wanted to play basketball with some new boy, but I was afraid he'd make fun of me because, in fact, I stink at basketball?"

"Something like that. What would you do?"

"I'd put itching powder into his gym shorts."

Some help he was. We had reached Kaspar Snit's front door. Solly was about to knock, when the door opened from the inside.

There stood Levon du Plessy-Minsk. And right beside him was Fox.

"My, my," said Levon du Plessy-Minsk. "It's the Blande children, I believe. Fox, isn't this girl in your class?"

"Yes," he said, looking miserable.

"What are you doing here?" I asked.

"We were just consulting with Mr. Parsstinka about the Mysterious Flying Girl," said Fox's father. "After all, he is a science teacher."

Levon du Plessy-Minsk swung the door all the way open to reveal Kaspar Snit looking very uncomfortable. "Mr. Parsstinka, you have been most helpful. Now, if you will excuse us, Fox and I have work to do. We're hot on the trail!"

Solly and I stepped aside as Levon du Plessy-Minsk put on his pith helmet and came out the door. Fox looked at me as if to say *Dads are so embarrassing*. But I couldn't even smile and just watched them get into the minivan and drive away, the radar detector turning on the roof.

Solly and I went into the house. Even before Kaspar Snit closed the door, I said, "What were they doing here?"

"Yeah, and don't tell us that you're starting a knitting club," Solly said.

"I couldn't help it," Kaspar Snit said, holding out his arms helplessly. "He knocked on my door. I had to let them in. He wanted to know about the aerodynamic possibilities of teenage girls. He showed me his map."

"And what did you tell him?"

"Really, Eleanor, what do you think I told him? I said that I don't believe that humans can fly."

"Maybe we shouldn't believe you," Solly said. "You might be in a caboose with him."

"You mean in cahoots," Kaspar Snit said. "You'll just have to trust me. Come into the living room. See what I've bought? This proves I want to be a regular person."

We followed him in and he pointed with pride towards a rather ordinary-looking coffee table. "I've never had one before," he said. "It's extremely useful. You can put things on it. Like, well, like . . ."

"Coffee?" Solly said.

"Exactly."

"And how about cookies – hint, hint."

"Oh, yes, I've got them right in the kitchen. Stay here. It's quite fun being ordinary. I'm thinking of getting a blender next. Here are the cookies. Enjoy!"

He put the plate down on the coffee table as well as the box they came from. The cookies were small and dry-looking, with a purple spot in the center. On the box it said TWEEZNIT'S PRUNE BISCUITS, EAT THEM REGULARLY AND YOU'LL BE REGULAR! Solly picked one up, sniffed it, and took a bite.

"That's the worst cookie I've ever tasted," he said, putting the other half down. "Eating one is a punishment, not a treat. Eleanor, I think we should change one of our lessons to 'Choose cookies that kids will actually like.'"

"There isn't time. Today Kaspar Snit has to write a poem."

"This lesson ought to be a piece of cake," Kaspar Snit said, rubbing his hands together.

"Please," Solly said. "Don't mention cake."

But writing a poem turned out to be not so easy, at least not for Kaspar Snit. First of all, he couldn't think of a subject, not one that he thought would make a good poem. Solly and I consulted and decided to suggest a topic. "How about Mrs. Leer?" I said. "After all, there are lots of poems about love."

Kaspar Snit liked that idea. If the poem came out well, he said, then he could give it to her. But how was he to actually write a poem? He'd written television scripts, but that was different. Rhyming was so hard. I told him that my English teacher showed us that modern poems didn't have to rhyme, but Kaspar Snit insisted that would be cheating. Finally he said that he couldn't possibly write while I was staring at him and Solly was arranging the prune biscuits into a pyramid. So we agreed to come back after dinner and see what he had accomplished.

But we didn't have to go back. Kaspar Snit came to us instead. "I've done it – I've written a poem!" he exclaimed, while we were still having dessert. So while Solly, Mom, Dad, and I sat at the table, he recited to us his "Ode to Lucretia Leer."

You are not young, you are not old.
You do not like Swiss cheese with mold.
Instead you'd rather have a beer.
You are the wondrous Widow Leer.

Of tin-whistle tooters, there is no finer.
Your chicken marshmallow could not be diviner.
A caregiver giant without peer,
You are the wondrous Widow Leer.

I am a scoundrel, bum, and cad.
My deeds till now have been awfully bad.
But the world has nothing more to fear
Because I'm nuts for the Widow Leer.

I know how much it makes you teary
To think of the one you call dear and dreary.
But a plea of mercy would you hear
From one love-struck by the Widow Leer?

My poem is done, for I'm out of rhymes,
And this verse is worse than my worstest crimes.
Put me in jail forever and a year
If I cannot win the Widow Leer.

When Kaspar Snit finished, looking up from his paper, face pale and lips trembling, we all applauded.

"Bravo! First-rate!" Dad said.

"Really?" Kaspar Snit looked at us with relief. "But do you think it could win her heart? You are a woman, Daisy. Would it win yours?"

"Well," Mom said, "if I were a different person, under different circumstances, and with different tastes – then yes, it certainly would."

"Thank you," Kaspar Snit said, lowering his head. "You give me hope."

On Thursday we met Kaspar Snit at the bus stop for lesson six, and the three of us headed for the main street in town. "I don't understand why I need a pet," Kaspar Snit said, as the bus lurched forward. "I don't like animals. I don't think they're cute. I don't get all warm and fuzzy when I see a puppy."

"That's the whole point," I said. "We need to soften your edges. We need to bring out the warm and gooey side of you, Kaspar."

"Yeah," Solly said. "Just look what having my rat, G.W., has done for me. Aren't I so sweet now? Here, you can hold him."

Because Solly wasn't wearing his Googoo-man outfit anymore, he didn't have a cape with a pocket to carry G.W. Instead, he wore an old Barney knapsack with airholes poked into it, and now he swung it off his shoulder and scooped out his rat. G.W. lifted up his head to sniff the air.

"Please keep that disease-carrying sock puppet away from me," Kaspar Snit said.

"But he's *sooo* cute," Solly said, in a baby voice.

I guess the man sitting next to G.W. didn't think he was so cute. Because when he saw the rat, he started to scream. A moment later, five or six other people were screaming too as they pushed their way to the back of the bus. The bus driver put on the brakes, then came down the aisle to see what all the fuss was about.

We walked the rest of the way to the pet shop.

"Rats," Solly said, as we trudged along the street, "are a misunderstood species."

"In about a minute," I said, "you're going to be an extinct species."

At last we got to the pet shop, a small corner store crowded with cages and aquariums, kitty-litter bags and dog food, and noisy with the sound of screeching birds. Solly and I began to show Kaspar Snit around.

"Look at those adorable guinea pigs," Solly said.

"In their native country, people roast them on spits," Kaspar Snit said. "They are said to be delicious."

"Okay, forget the guinea pigs," I said. "How about a parakeet?"

Kaspar Snit looked at the cage of beautifully colored birds. "They remind me of the time you covered me with feathers," he said.

"You can't have anything bad to say about these," Solly said.

Kaspar Snit and I turned to see a large aquarium of goldfish. They were swimming in such a leisurely way, they looked as if they were on vacation.

"Oh, aren't they fascinating," Kaspar Snit sneered. "What do I do with them? Have fish races? See how many can fit into a sardine can?"

"You can't dislike everything," I said. "I mean, the whole point is to –" But I stopped talking, for I had just seen the corners of Kaspar Snit's eyes go all crinkly.

"There! That's it! That's my pet!" he cried.

He was pointing to a small glass terrarium. Peering in, I could only see some bark on the bottom and a few dead branches. I was going to say that there was nothing in there, when suddenly I saw something.

Big.

Hairy.

Eight-legged.

"A tarantula?" Solly said. "That is *so* cool."

"No, no, no." I shook my head. "We're trying to make Kaspar Snit into a regular person, remember? He can't have a pet just to creep people out."

"I disagree," Kaspar Snit said. "Look how fuzzy and cute he is. I already feel close to that fellow. There's no point in my getting a pet if I don't like it, is there?"

I sighed. "I guess so. After all, you'll still have to take care of it."

"Good," Kaspar Snit said. "And I already have a name for it."

"What?" Solly asked.

Kaspar Snit grinned. "Lawrence."

"Lawrence?" I said. "You've got to be kidding."

"Don't listen to their insults, Lawrence," Kaspar Snit said, leaning towards the glass. "Let's you and me go home."

Kaspar Snit bought the tarantula, the terrarium, stuff for the bottom, and a dozen crickets to feed it. We took a cab home, and Solly and I watched Kaspar Snit get his new pet settled. He put the terrarium on top of the coffee table, still the only piece of furniture in the living room.

"Welcome home, Lawrence," Kaspar Snit said.

The tarantula waved one hairy leg in the air.

On Friday after school, Solly and I went straight to Kaspar Snit's house. "You know," he said, letting us inside, "these lessons aren't so tough after all. I'm even enjoying them. Before yesterday I was living alone, with nobody but myself to talk to. And now I can talk to Lawrence. I come downstairs and say, 'Good morning, Lawrence. Did you sleep well?' Just before leaving the house, I say, 'See you later, Lawrence. Don't get into any mischief.' And when I come home, I say, 'I hope you didn't miss me too much, Lawrence.' It's a lot better than talking to the coffee table. So what's on for today?"

"Today," I said, "you have to take care of a baby."

Kaspar Snit chortled through his nose. "That's a good one. A baby! I suppose you've brought me some plastic doll that I have to pretend to feed and carry. Ah, well, if I must, I must."

"We don't have any plastic doll," Solly said.

"Then do we get to skip this one? I'm sure one less lesson won't hurt."

The doorbell rang. "Must be a special delivery," I said.

"But I didn't order anything."

I went towards the door. "No, but we did." Kaspar Snit and Solly both followed me, and I opened the door to a woman with dark hair piled high on her head, a chunky ceramic necklace, and vibrant red lipstick.

She was holding a baby. A big, red-cheeked baby, blowing bubbles out of the corner of his mouth and waving his chubby hands. He was completely bald and wore a cute little sailor suit.

"Hi, Mrs. Doovis," I said.

"Eleanor! It's so nice to see you. And I'm so excited! This will be my first time out of the house in six months. It's so good of you to arrange for Mr. Parsstinka to baby-sit for me. And *you* must be the teacher who replaced me. Mr. Parsstinka, I was delighted to hear that you are wonderful with babies. I'm just *so* grateful."

Kaspar Snit didn't say a word. He was too stunned. He stared at the woman, eyes large, mouth frozen half-open as if he was trying to say something. I said, "Mr. Parsstinka, this is my old teacher, Mrs. Doovis. You know, the one who is staying home because she had a baby."

"Ah . . . ah. . . ." Kaspar Snit tried to speak.

"Of course you're speechless," Mrs. Doovis said. "He is the most adorable thing, isn't he? You're just a sweetie pie, aren't you, Julius? Let Momma wipe that drool off your face. Nice Mr. Parsstinka here is going to take care of you for the next four hours while Momma exercises at the gym and goes to a movie."

"Did you say *four hours*?" Kaspar Snit managed to say.

"I know you'd like to have Julius for longer, but it'll be time for his beddy-byes. Here you go, Mr. Parsstinka," she said, thrusting the baby into Kaspar Snit's arms. "And here is the bag of all his things. Baby food, bottles, wipes, and, of course, plenty of diapers. He hasn't made his poo-poo yet. Well, I better say *ta-ta* before Julius realizes that he's being abandoned. I wouldn't be surprised if he cries at the top of his lungs for an hour or so. Have fun!"

And before we had a chance to say good-bye, she was hurrying down the steps of the porch, crying, "I'm free, I'm free!"

Solly and I turned to look at Kaspar Snit, who looked down at the baby. The baby looked back. It reached out its little hand and grabbed Kaspar Snit's nose.

"Nice daydee," Kaspar Snit said, through his pinched nose. "Not doo hard now."

Gently, Kaspar Snit pulled Julius's hand from his nose. The baby smiled. Then he shifted his eyes to the left. No mother. He shifted his eyes to the right. No mother there, either.

"*Waaaaah!*"

"You are going to help, aren't you?" Kaspar Snit pleaded.

"That," Solly said, "would be cheating."

HEAVY

LIFTING

Those four hours must have been the longest in Kaspar Snit's life. When Mrs. Doovis finally returned, the baby was happy, smelling fresh, and in a clean new outfit. But Kaspar Snit was covered in mashed carrots and peas. They were stuck to his clothes, in his hair, even in that mustache that little Julius so liked to yank.

"Oh, Mr. Parsstinka," Mrs. Doovis said, as Kaspar Snit practically tossed the baby into her arms, "you don't know how grateful I am. Those four hours have done me a world of good. And look how happy my precious Julius is. He's really taken to you, I can tell. You have a natural way with infants. Well, it's off to sleepy-times. Say good-bye to Uncle Parsstinka."

Kaspar Snit closed the door behind her and slumped against it. "I've never been so tired in my life," he said. "And now, if the two of you will leave me, I'm going to take a bath and go to bed. I can only hope that I shall be recovered in time for school on Monday. But you know what?"

"What?" I asked.

"I, myself, find it hard to believe, but he was kind of cute."

On Saturday morning, everybody got up late. I had breakfast by myself in the kitchen, eating cereal and reading the color comics in the newspaper. Then I went to Solly's room and gently pushed open the door, in case he was sleeping. But he wasn't sleeping; he was sitting on the floor, with G.W. on his shoulder and his personal photo album in his lap, looking at the pictures: Googoo-man with his hair standing up from static electricity at the Science Museum; Googoo-man missing a fly ball in center field during a Little League game; Googoo-man holding up two hamburgers as if they were heavy weights outside of a highway diner. He looked up at me. "Yup, those were good times," he said.

A nine-year-old kid, and already he was nostalgic for his youth. I was going to try and snap him out of it, but something interrupted me – a terrible grinding and ripping noise that was coming from outside. And not just noise; the whole house was shaking.

"Is that an earthquake?" Solly asked, grabbing G.W.

"I don't think so," I said. "Quick, let's look outside."

I started to run even before Solly was off the floor. I sprinted down the hall, the ground trembling beneath me, and threw open the front door. Solly pushed up behind me.

"Holy tomato!" Solly said.

It was no earthquake, but an enormous flatbed truck with a crane on it. Chains from the crane were wrapped around our fountain, which had just been torn up from the ground. I could see bits of marble falling from the base and broken pipes sticking out of the earth.

"Dad! Mom!" I screamed. "Our fountain! Our fountain's being stolen again!"

A moment later, Mom and Dad came up behind us, wrapped in blankets. They, too, looked out the doorway at the crane, which was swiveling towards the flatbed.

"It isn't being stolen," Dad said.

"It's not?"

"No. It's been sold."

"What do you mean, sold?" Solly asked.

Dad put his hand on Solly's shoulder and then on mine. "I'm sorry, kids. We need the money to make the payments on the house. With no work coming in these days, I'm not bringing in any income. It was a hard decision, but we really have no choice."

"Oh, Manfred," Mom said, her voice choked up. "It's just the most awful sight."

We all watched as the crane lowered the fountain onto the flatbed with a tremendous thud. Two men in overalls came out of the truck cab and tied the fountain down with ropes.

"Where is it going?" I asked.

"To a shopping mall in New Jersey. At Christmas, they're putting elf caps on the statues."

The two men got back into the truck cab. Black smoke poured from the exhaust, the gears roared, and a moment later, the truck drove away. Only when it was gone did I notice all the other people looking out their windows and front doors.

Dad ignored them. He went to the side of the house and came back with a heavy mallet. He knocked the pipes flat and then he brought out bags of earth and covered our front lawn. Next he brought out a flat of begonias and planted them here and there. When he was done, he retreated into his garage and, for a long time, we heard his mandolin softly playing, its broken string rattling.

Mom, Solly, and I stayed there looking at our front lawn, which now looked like everybody else's. "I already miss our fountain," I said.

"Me, too," Solly said. "Maybe we can buy it back. I have three dollars and twenty-three cents saved up."

"I don't think that's going to do it," Mom said.

"We could have a lemonade stand on Saturday."

"Solly, the fountain is worth thousands of dollars."

"Oh," Solly said. He turned around and went back into the house. Mom went after him, but I stayed there. I used to like begonias. But I didn't like them anymore.

FOR WHOM
THE BELL TOLLS

All weekend, the only thing I could think about was our fountain being gone. It was a good thing that Kaspar Snit had asked for a break because I needed one just as much. On the way to school on Monday, I was sure that all the kids and teachers were looking at me, and maybe even feeling sorry for me, and I hated the thought. I was at my locker when Julia Worthington came up and said, "Eleanor, I'm really sorry –" but I cut her off and ran to my next class.

After school, Solly and I went right home, where we found my dad at the kitchen table with the newspaper WANT ADS spread over the table. He was using a purple crayon to circle job opportunities that he might apply for. "'Shampoo artist for hair salon,'" he read aloud. "*Hmm*. I know how to shampoo my own hair. Or how about this one? 'Fortune cookie writer.' Or, 'Golf ball washer.' Hey, aren't you two supposed to be giving Kaspar Snit his next lesson?"

"In a few minutes," I said. "He gave some kids a detention for putting glue in his shoes."

"How did they manage to put glue in his shoes?"

"Sometimes he takes them off and falls asleep at his desk. I don't think he's really cut out to be a teacher. Dad?" I said.

"Yes, Eleanor?"

"I don't feel much like giving him a lesson today. Maybe we can skip it."

My dad pushed aside the newspaper. For the first time this afternoon, he really looked at me. "Are you feeling bad about the fountain?" he asked.

"Bad?" Solly said. "We feel awful. I guess we got used to having eight naked butts on our front lawn."

"Come here," Dad said. We came over and he put an arm around each of us. "I'm really touched that you miss it. Of course I do too, and so does Mom. But we're still a great family, right? We're still the Galinski Blande clan. Now I want you to go and give Kaspar Snit a heck of a lesson. He needs it."

Somehow Dad made me feel a little better. We said goodbye, grabbed a cookie each from a dish on the counter (not trusting Kaspar Snit to have any worth eating), and headed outside.

And saw Fox, from my class, coming up the walk. My heart jumped.

Fox stopped. "Hi," he said. "I was just coming to your door."

"You were?" I said.

Solly narrowed his eyes at Fox. "So what do you want with my sister anyway?"

"I just had a question about school."

"Do you think my sister's hot?"

"Solly, get out of here!" I shouted. "Go over to Kas – I mean, Mr. Parsstinka's house. I'll be there in a minute."

"Okay, okay. But hurry up."

Fox and I watched him saunter off, raising one shoulder and then another in a silly walk meant to make us laugh. Fox said, "Why are you going over to Mr. Parsstinka's house?"

"For some, uh, extra work."

"You must really like science."

"Sure. It's very, you know, scientific." I sounded like an idiot. "So, what are you doing here?" I asked.

"I was just kind of on the street. Well, six blocks away, actually. Would you maybe want to get a whipped caramel-chocolatino drink with me sometime?"

I wanted to say yes, but I remembered who Fox's father was. *How could I have a whipped caramel-chocolatino drink with the son of the man who wanted to display me and charge for tickets?*

Fox saw me hesitate because he said, "Hey, don't worry about it. It's cool if you don't want to. I'll see you in class." He turned around.

"No, wait," I called, but I'd hesitated too long and he was already running down the sidewalk. I watched him go, wishing that we were still talking. Then I walked the few houses over to Kaspar Snit's.

Crossing the street, I saw that Solly was on the porch, talking to a policeman. *What could that be about?* I hurried over, realizing that the policeman was the same one that Mrs. Leer and I had gone to when Solly had been captured in Misery Mountain – the same one who hadn't believed us then, but who later arrested Kaspar Snit, telling a lot of bad jokes in the process. He and Solly were examining Kaspar Snit's bicycle.

"Well, hello again," the policeman said. "Do you remember me? Officer Yogis. You've both grown since the last time we met."

"And you've lost more hair," said Solly.

"Solly!" I said.

"It's true enough," the man chuckled. "I imagine that you and your family are going to the opening of the State Treasures of Verulia exhibit?"

"Yes, we are," Solly said. "We got special invitations."

"Solly," I said, "don't brag."

"I'm not bragging. I'm showing off."

"Be sure to say hello to me. I'm going to be right at the front door. However, I'm here on another matter. Are you familiar with this bicycle?"

"Sure," I said. "It belongs to Mr. Parsstinka."

Officer Yogis leaned down and whispered, "That's all right, I know his real name. Kaspar Snit came to the police station voluntarily. Told us he was moving into the neighborhood. Wanted to be a good citizen and all that. Which shows that he has either truly changed his ways, or he is even more devilishly clever than we thought." He stood up straight again. "Now, Mr. Solly, if you would be so kind as to knock on the door."

But he didn't have to because, at that moment, the door opened and there was Kaspar Snit. "I was wondering where you two were. Oh, Officer Yogis, I didn't see you. Is there something I can help you with?"

"Yes, Mr. Parsstinka," he said, with a wink. "But first a joke. Knock, knock."

"Must I?" Kaspar Snit asked.

"Indulge me," Officer Yogis said.

"All right, who's there?"

"Abel."

"Abel who?"

"Abel is a good thing to have on a bicycle. Get it? *A bell?* As for the reason I'm here, may I ask if that is your bicycle?"

"It is. I can show you the receipt."

"Very good. I was noticing the bell."

"I believe it is a necessary piece of safety equipment," Kaspar Snit said.

"Quite right. But what interests me is, last night somebody stole all the bicycle bells in town. Every last one of them."

"Wow," said Solly. "That's a lot of bells."

"Yes, it is. All except this one. Peculiar, don't you think?"

Kaspar Snit stared at the bell on his own bike. "Yes, I admit it is."

"I mean," Officer Yogis went on, "why would a thief steal every bell except this one? That's the puzzle."

"Are you suggesting that I stole them?"

"Are you suggesting that you didn't?"

"I don't like your tone, Officer."

"Perhaps you don't, but the real question is, does it have the ring of truth? Get it? *Ring?* Stealing bicycle bells is a crime and an act of mischief. Just like that raid on the birthday party the other day. 'Who would bother?' I ask myself. And I answer myself, 'Perhaps someone who just wants a taste of being bad.'"

"Why don't you search my house? I give you permission. Look under the bed; look in the attic. See if you find any bells."

"I don't imagine the person who stole them would stick them all under his bed," Officer Yogis said.

"I insist that you come in anyway," Kaspar Snit said, opening the door wide. "Step right in. You can search every nook and cranny of the house. Why don't we start with the closet here? I'll just open it and show –" Kaspar Snit opened the closet door. Out spilled dozens – no, *hundreds* – of bicycle bells, chiming crazily as they rolled onto the floor and around our feet. More poured from the closet.

"My, my," said Officer Yogis. "What have we here?"

"I don't understand it," Kaspar Snit sputtered, staring at the bells around his feet. "I don't know how they got in there."

"Why?" said the officer. "Did you hide them somewhere else?"

"No, no, I didn't hide them at all. I mean, I didn't steal them."

Officer Yogis picked up a bell and pushed the lever to make it ring. "Well, this looks like pretty hard evidence to me. As the poet said, Mr. Snit, do not ask for whom the bell tolls. It tolls for none other than you. I'm going to have to take you in."

I felt so disappointed that I had to look away from Kaspar Snit. He had been trying so hard, and Solly and I had put so much effort into teaching him.

"If you take me in," Kaspar Snit said, backing towards the open door, "I won't be able to find out who is doing this. I need to know. I need to clear my name."

Kaspar backed through the front door and onto the porch. Officer Yogis said, "Now, now, don't do whatever it is you're thinking. Resisting arrest will just make things worse."

But Kaspar Snit didn't listen. He turned, grabbed his bike, pushed it forward, and hopped onto it as it bounced down the porch steps. His long feet flailed in the air before finding the pedals and, a moment later, he was cycling down the road.

I looked at Solly, who looked wide-eyed back at me.

"Are you going to go after him?" I asked the officer.

"With these flat feet?" Officer Yogis said. "I'll never catch him. But I'm not worried. I'll radio the station and all the police officers in town will be looking for him. He won't go far. I'm afraid it looks like Kaspar Snit is going back to jail. You get yourselves home now," he said, touching his cap. "I've got a criminal to catch."

Officer Yogis pulled the door shut and walked down to the road. He must not have been very concerned about being able to catch Kaspar Snit because he whistled as he headed along the sidewalk.

"What do you think?" Solly said to me. "Did Kaspar really do it?"

"I don't know. But I'm worried about him. And now where is he going to go? He'll be in even more trouble."

"Yeah. Running away – well, bicycling away – was a bad idea."

"Boy this is weird," I said. "We're actually worrying about Kaspar Snit. . . ."

"I know." Solly nodded. "It's making me nauseous. I need to go home and have some ice cream."

"We can't just go home," I said. "We've got some responsibility here now. I mean, Kaspar Snit is our pupil, isn't he?"

"Sure. But what can we do?"

"Follow him."

"How can we follow him? He's long gone. By the time we get our bikes out of the garage . . ."

"Hello? Aren't you forgetting something? We can *fly*."

"You're the one who's against flying during the day. What if somebody sees us?"

"Nobody better see us. We have to hurry, or we'll never find him. Let's go around to the backyard. We can take off from there."

Solly nodded eagerly and the two of us raced around to the back. Kaspar Snit hadn't done anything to keep it up – the grass needed cutting and dandelion weeds bloomed everywhere. Solly plucked a dandelion and held it under his chin.

"Do I like butter?" he said.

"Put that down; we don't have time." I placed my hands at my sides and Solly did the same. Trying to fly during the day made me feel strangely exposed, but I closed my eyes, thought *up,* and, a moment later, I was hovering over Kaspar Snit's house with Solly rising after me.

"Let's get higher, so we won't be seen," I said.

We both rose higher, which also had the advantage of giving us a wider view of the ground below. Hovering, I scanned the surrounding streets, searching for a man in a cape on a bicycle, but I couldn't see him. Then Solly said, "Over there! Going past Schmelling's Grocery," and, sure enough, I could see Kaspar Snit pedaling away.

"Let's go," I said. "And remember to keep moving."

Following Kaspar Snit wasn't as easy as it sounded. For one thing, our natural flying speed was about three times faster than his was on a bike, so we had to make sure not to overtake him. For another, Kaspar Snit had to follow the roads, turning left at one corner, right at another, cutting through an alley. We had to zigzag through the sky.

Kaspar Snit pedaled on, past the water tower on the outskirts of town and then the hockey arena. "Where in the heck is he going?" Solly said. I didn't know the answer, not until he pulled into the empty parking lot of Rooster's Fried Chicken and leaned his bike against the fence.

"He wants a snack? The police are after him and he needs an order of famous fatty fries?"

"Let's go down," I said. "We better make it quick if we don't want to be seen."

A fast landing was always risky. I had to pull up in time so as not to crash into the ground. So far, the worst that had ever happened to me was a sprained ankle, but I was always worried about breaking something. Now I made my steepest descent ever, plunging almost straight down and reversing my thoughts at only fifteen feet above the pavement. My feet hit hard, but I kept my knees flexed and managed to absorb the shock and keep standing.

Kaspar Snit turned and looked at me in surprise. "Eleanor! What are you doing here?"

A moment later Solly came down, somersaulted past us, and smacked into the fence beside Kaspar Snit's bicycle.

"Solly, are you all right?" I said, running up to him.

"I'm fine," he said, wobbling as he got up. "A little dizzy, that's all. It was kind of fun."

I turned back to Kaspar Snit, who had followed me over to Solly. "Do you really think running away from the policeman was the right thing to do?"

Kaspar Snit shook his head. "Maybe not. But if I'm in jail, how can I prove my innocence?"

"Okay, but why Rooster's Fried Chicken?" I said. "It's not even open. My dad and I tried to go the other day."

We turned and looked at the building. All of the windows had plywood sheets over them and there was a CLOSED FOR RENOVATIONS sign nailed by the take-out window.

"I came because of this," Kaspar Snit said. He reached into a pocket in his cape and pulled out a crumpled sheet of paper. "Somebody put it in my mailbox. I found it when I came home today, just before that policeman arrived."

Kaspar Snit held out the paper. I took it and smoothed it out. Someone had cut letters out from newspapers and magazines, pasting them down to make words.

IF YOU WANT To KNOw
COME TO
ROOSTER'S FRIED CHICKEN

"If you want to know?" Solly said, looking over my shoulder. "Want to know what?"

"Who is pretending to be me," Kaspar Snit said. "Who dares to wear a cape and mustache. Who put those bells in my closet to make me look guilty."

"But you can't just walk in there," I said. "I mean, it could be a trap. Otherwise, why would someone send you an anonymous note?"

"Good thinking," Kaspar Snit said. "And with all the windows boarded up, we can't see what – or who – is inside."

"I know what we should do," Solly said. "Go to the roof."

"The roof?"

"Uh-huh. You know that giant metal rooster up on the roof? When you're inside the restaurant, you can look up through the open skylight and see through the rooster's mouth. That means we should be able to look down the mouth and see into the restaurant. They only close it when it's raining."

"That is an excellent suggestion," Kaspar Snit said. "I am impressed, young Solly. The only problem is, how do we get onto the roof?"

"Elementary, my dear Snit," Solly answered. "We fly."

"Well, that may be the answer for you, but it hardly helps me."

"We can bring you up," I said. "All you have to do is, wait till we're a few feet in the air and then grab on to our legs. It isn't too far, so we should be able to carry you."

"Is this another lesson in telling a joke? You really expect me to hang on to you while you rise fifty feet in the air?"

"Do you see another solution?" I asked. "You have to learn to trust people, Kaspar."

Kaspar Snit grimaced. "All right," he said. "But no fooling around. No trying to scare me for fun."

"Hey, we're the ones who are going to be doing all the work," Solly said. "How about a thank-you?"

Kaspar Snit sighed. "Yes, you are right. Thank you. Now let's get it over with."

Solly and I nodded to one another. We stood side by side, got into position, and I instructed Kaspar Snit to stand behind us. "We have to rise as slowly as possible," I told Solly, "so that Kaspar Snit can grab on. Then we'll accelerate. I'll count to three." We both closed our eyes and I counted softly, "One . . . two . . . three," and let myself rise as gently as a leaf on a breeze. A moment later, I felt Kaspar Snit's hand grasp my ankle – hard. *Ugh!* I heard Solly groan as his ankle got grabbed too. Aloud I said, "Now!" and we both boosted our energy and rose upwards, fighting the drag caused by Kaspar Snit. My eyes opened and I watched the brickwork of Rooster's Fried Chicken slide past as I headed up towards the roof.

"This is most undignified," Kaspar Snit said.

"*You* don't feel dignified?" Solly said. "You're pulling down my pants!"

"Just one more minute," I called out. We rose past the top edge of the building and then hovered over the flat gravel-and-tar roof. "Now let go."

"But I'll fall," Kaspar Snit whimpered.

"Yeah, about three inches," Solly said. Kaspar Snit released his grip, but while he tumbled down, we suddenly shot upwards as if flung out of a slingshot. Solly did a loop, but I just spiraled back down to the roof, landing beside Kaspar Snit, who was brushing off his knees.

"I did not enjoy that," Kaspar Snit said.

"Sorry, no refund on ride tickets," Solly said.

"So what do we do now?" I asked. "Look down the mouth of the rooster?"

"That, apparently, is the idea," Kaspar Snit said.

We all turned to the rooster behind us. It was a good twelve feet tall, made of painted metal, with yellow feet, spread-out wings, and a big red rooster's comb on the head. The beak was open and the head arched back, like it was cock-a-doodle-doing the whole town awake. I was about to suggest that Solly or I fly up to the beak and take a look down, when I heard a shout.

"Stay where you are!"

The shout came from someone who was climbing on top of the rooster's head. It was Levon du Plessy-Minsk!

"I've got it! I've got it all recorded!" he shouted, and I saw that he was holding a camera. "The Mysterious Flying Girl, captured for all to see! And it's none other than Eleanor Blande. And, lo and behold, a Mysterious Flying Boy too. I've got full shots, close-ups, the works. That one-thousand-and-ten-dollar reward is mine. Not to mention fame. I'll no longer be known as the man who didn't find the Loch Ness Monster, or the man who missed Big Foot. Oh, this is good, this is very, very good!" Levon du Plessy-Minsk wiggled with triumph as he sat atop the rooster.

I felt ill. *What would happen to us when everybody knew we could fly? Would we have to leave Inkpotts Public School? Would we have to change our names and move to another country?*

"How did you get up here anyway?" Solly asked.

"Simple. There's a ladder on the other side of the building and steps behind the rooster."

Kaspar Snit looked at me – we'd never even checked! He said to the creature catcher, "So you left me that note to come here. To trick me."

"Note? I don't know about any note. I saw those two people flying and followed in my minivan."

Kaspar Snit frowned. "Mr. du Plessy-Minsk, think of these children for a moment. If you expose them, they will be hounded by newspaper and television reporters. People will stare and point and follow them with cameras. They will be treated as odd, even freakish. Is it worth it? Just for a little fame? I, too, longed for fame once. I know all too well that little worm that gnaws at your insides, that is never satisfied. You will ruin their lives and not even make yourself happy. I'm sure that you can find some generosity in your heart. Won't you erase the recording, Mr. du Plessy-Minsk?"

"He's right, Dad," came a voice from behind the rooster. Out stepped . . . Fox! *He was here too?* I felt my face go beet red.

"Hey, Eleanor," he said, giving me a little wave.

"Hey, Fox."

"Nice flying."

"Thanks."

"Son," his father said sharply, as he looked down. "I told you to stay behind the rooster."

"It isn't fair, Dad," Fox said. "We don't have any right to tell the world they can fly. You always taught me to treat people decently."

"People, yes. But not creatures."

"But they aren't creatures. They *are* people. I want you to give me the camera, so I can erase what you took." Fox reached up to his father.

"Never!" his father cried, clutching the camera to his chest. "I'll never give it up."

Holding the camera so tightly, the creature catcher had let go of the rooster's head. He began to slip down the open beak! *"Yeeaow!"* he cried, his scream fading as he disappeared inside.

"Dad!" cried Fox. "Oh, no. He might have hurt himself. I've got to get inside."

"But the door is locked," I said. "And the windows are boarded up too."

"Yeah," Solly said. "There's something in there. Something that likes birthday cake and bicycle bells. Something bad."

"I've got to help my dad. I guess there's only one way."

Fox disappeared behind the rooster. A moment later, he reappeared on top of the rooster's head. He was going to follow his father down. "Fox, don't!" I said, but he didn't listen. He swung himself over the top and into the rooster's mouth.

"Look out belowww. . . ." His voice faded away.

Solly and Kaspar Snit and I looked from one to the other. We couldn't just let Fox and his father go in there alone, but what were we supposed to do?

Kaspar Snit said, "That note came for no one but me. That young lad has put himself in jeopardy to help his father, but I am the one who this fiend has been trying to lure in. It is time that I came face-to-face with my adversary."

Solly clapped enthusiastically. "That was a really good speech."

Kaspar Snit threw his cape over his shoulder and marched behind the rooster. Solly and I followed him and saw the metal steps that ran up the rooster's back.

Kaspar Snit climbed up, his elbows and knees sticking out, and when he came to the top, he eased himself into the rooster's open beak, holding his nose as if he were about to plunge into a swimming pool. As he began to slide down, we could hear clanging against metal and a few *ow*'s and *ah*'s. Then nothing.

"There's no way that G.W. and I are getting left behind," Solly said, and he scampered up the metal steps.

"Solly, no! We should be the sensible ones, at least. As your older sister, I order you to come back down."

"And as your younger brother, I say *blahh!*" He stuck out his tongue.

Growling under my breath, I hurried to catch him, springing up the steps. Just as he made for the open beak, I lunged forward, trying to grab hold of his knapsack straps. I got them all right, but I tumbled headlong after him.

Solly and I slid down the chute together, my elbows growing hot against the metal. Before I even had a chance to yelp, we were dropping out the bottom onto something soft and bouncy. It was a mattress.

"*Ow!* Get your foot out of my ear," Solly said.

It took a moment before we could untangle ourselves and begin to see what was around us. In the dim light cast by a couple of overhead bulbs, I could see Kaspar Snit, along with Levon du Plessy-Minsk and Fox, standing beside the mattress and shaking themselves off. Around us in the dark were the tables and plastic chairs of the restaurant. There was a long counter at one end, with the menu above it, and the fryers and other cooking equipment visible behind. The only thing really different was that, with all the windows boarded up and almost no light coming in, the place felt pretty creepy.

Levon du Plessy-Minsk finished straightening his pith helmet. He still held the camera in his hand. "Come on, Fox," he said, "we've got to get this video to the television station for the evening news. Well, it was nice spending time with the rest of you, but we have to go."

"But, Dad," Fox said.

"Right now," he said, striding towards the door. He turned the knob, but the door didn't open. "Very peculiar," he grumbled, yanking it. "Somebody has locked it with a key. There must be some way out of here."

"Perhaps I can help you."

The voice made all of us turn. In the dark I could see a figure standing on the counter, feet apart, hands on hips. A figure in a black cape, with the curling ends of a mustache just visible. *Kaspar Snit! But how could that be, when Kaspar Snit was standing next to me?* We all looked from one to the other and back again. Even Kaspar Snit – the one beside me – stared at the figure on the counter in disbelief.

Solly said, "It isn't Halloween, is it?"

"There aren't going to be any treats, if that's what you mean," said the figure.

"Who are you?" Kaspar Snit said. "I demand to know."

"Do you, boss?" The figure started to laugh.

NEW GENIUS
IN TOWN

It wasn't the diabolical laughter of the old Kaspar Snit, though; it was more like the naughty giggling of a kid after you've sat on his whoopee cushion. He was about to leap dramatically down from the counter, when he changed his mind and sat down on the countertop, lowering himself from there. Then he came towards us.

"I'll show you who I am," he said, and he placed one hand on his face and the other on his head. "It is a real thrill to see you again." At that moment, he pulled his hands away, taking his hair and his mustache with them! Looking at the face now, with the bald head, round nose, small eyes, and the little tuft of hair under the lower lip, I gasped with recognition. So did Kaspar Snit beside me.

"Slouch!" Kaspar Snit cried. "I cannot believe it."

"That's right, boss, your former servant, your right-hand man, lackey, menial, drudge. The one who obeyed your every order, who smiled when you insulted him, who did all of the dirty work and got none of the glory. None other than Marvin Slouchovsky, otherwise known as just plain Slouch."

"But I thought you had gone back to acting. You were in the television show that replaced mine, the one where the family swam underwater."

"The Swoomers," Solly said. "Crummy show."

"Which is why it was canceled after half a season," Slouch said. "And you know how life is for an actor. I was out of work once again. But I've found a new line that suits me much better."

"And that is?" said Kaspar Snit.

"Why, haven't you guessed? I'm the new you! Look out, world, there's a new evil genius in town. When I heard you were going straight, I said to myself, 'Now there's a market niche, a financial opportunity, a consumer need waiting to be filled.' I learned a lot from watching you, Kaspar, old boy. I learned that being an evil genius is both satisfying and rewarding work."

"Then it was you who raided that kid's birthday party. And who stole those bicycle bells."

Slouch made a mock bow. "That was indeed yours truly."

"Boy, were those dumb," Solly said. "I mean, not to hurt your feelings, but Kaspar Snit would never have stooped so low."

"Thank you," Kaspar said.

"You're quite right. But they were just tastes, little appetizers of the meal to come. Getting the atmosphere right, you might say."

"But I do not understand," Kaspar Snit said. "Why did you imitate me? When I was evil, I wanted my name to be known far and wide. I wanted the glory of infamy. But nobody knows who you are."

"Exactly," Slouch said, and smiled. "You see, that's the one difference between us, boss. I had my taste of fame as an actor, and you know what? It's not all it's cracked up to be. I can live without it. Do you know what I really want?"

"What?" said Kaspar quietly.

"I'll tell you what. I want m-o-n-e-y. *Money.* Mansions and swimming pools and racing cars and servants and giant TVs. And that's why I'm going to succeed where you failed. Because the good guys aren't going to catch me. They're not even going to know who I am. They're going to think that what I am about to do is actually the work of someone else."

"Me," Kaspar Snit said grimly.

"Bingo!" said Slouch, with a grin. "Now, I'm sure all of you must be hungry after that ride down the rooster. Who would like some triple-fried chicken chunks with super-gloopy dipping sauce?"

Nobody felt like eating, but Slouch insisted on bringing out trays of food anyway – jumbo-sized super-sweet sodas, mounds of famous fatty fries, and lots of chicken chunks. It reminded me of the cooking that he did for us when Kaspar

Snit held us captive in Misery Mountain. Sure, Slouch had been Kaspar Snit's servant, but nobody had forced him. He'd thought that Kaspar was his ticket to success.

Kaspar Snit looked down on the food and sniffed contemptuously. "I don't understand," he said. "How is it you are using this grease-lover's paradise as your headquarters?"

"Maybe it isn't exactly your old fortress in Verulia, or even Misery Mountain," Slouch said. "But I call it home. You want to know the truth? After *The Swoomers* got canceled, I needed a job. I became a server here. Wore the paper hat, the apron. Had to say, 'Have a cock-a-doodle day!' after everybody's order. And then, when I came up with my plan and needed a headquarters, this seemed like just the place. Of course, the owner wasn't so keen on giving the restaurant up, so I had to swindle him out of it. It was so very naughty of me. I do hope you won't tell anyone."

"Okay," I said. "So now you're here. And you've been imitating Kaspar Snit so that the police suspect he's turning bad again. And you've lured him to your headquarters. But why?"

"Oh," Slouch said, wriggling his eyebrows. "It isn't just Kaspar Snit that I've lured here. It's you too, Eleanor."

"Me?"

"You're a crucial part of my scheme. Your brother is an added bonus. As for this dinosaur hunter and his son, I admit they were not in my plans. But as long as they stay out of my way, I'll make sure they don't get hurt."

Levon du Plessy-Minsk turned to his son. "Look what I've done," he said. "I've put you in danger, Fox. I was selfish. I didn't care about anyone but myself. I'm sorry."

"Don't sweat it, Dad," Fox said.

Levon du Plessy-Minsk turned to Slouch. "We weren't in your plans. Why don't you let my son and me go? We'll be in the way."

"Dad, we can't just leave the others here."

"*Shh,* son, let me take care of this. Mr. Slouch, you won't even know we were here."

"Don't you worry," Slouch said. "I'm sure I can find a use for you. Is that your minivan parked out back?"

"It is," Levon du Plessy-Minsk said.

"You can hand over the keys. Eleanor and I need it to get to the Constance Foote Museum of Art."

Fox's father fished the keys out of one of his vest pockets. "It's a little temperamental," he said. "If it stalls, you have to –"

"Hey, if anyone knows cars, it's me. Don't worry about it," Slouch said, grabbing the keys in his fist.

"The museum?" I said. "Why are we going to the museum? It's closed right now. They're putting in the . . . the . . ." I stopped speaking. My eyes grew wide.

"Yup, that's right," Slouch said. "They're putting in the new exhibit, ANCIENT SPLENDOR: GOLD, SILVER, JEWELRY, AND OTHER VALUABLE STUFF FROM THE STATE TREASURES OF VERULIA. And very soon, all that valuable stuff is going to belong to me. Pretty good, huh? Better than stealing crummy old fountains or kids' lunch money."

"You are no evil genius," Kaspar Snit said. "You are a mere criminal."

"You think so, do you? Well, I believe my plan is pretty smart. When the police discover the theft and look for the mastermind, they will naturally think of you. Especially as the sole eyewitness will describe someone who looks and dresses just like you."

"But I am trying to be good. I am a regular person now!"

"Just try and convince the police of that. I'm sure they'll be *very* sympathetic. Oh, I'm so excited! It feels like my birthday. I'm going to be rich, I'm going to be rich, I'm going to be rich. I hardly believe it. I could just pinch myself."

"How about I pinch you?" Solly said.

"Still the same obnoxious brat, I see. Well, I've got some last minute planning to do. I'll be in the kitchen, which is my office, so none of you try anything funny. Oh, and in case fly girl here or her brother has an idea to go back up the way they came, don't waste your time."

Slouch got up onto the counter and closed a wooden hatch over the bottom of the chute we had slid down. He slipped a lock onto it, turned the key, and dropped the key into his pocket. Then he got down again and went into the kitchen. But he didn't look like he was working. He was stuffing triple-fried chicken chunks into his mouth.

And here I'd thought that thirteen was going to be my best year ever. Instead, it was turning out to be a total disaster.

Not only was Dad unemployed, Mom afraid to fly, Solly an ex-superhero, and Kaspar Snit a pathetic, love-struck former evil genius, but now an entire country's heritage needed saving. Besides, H. Waldorf Mansfield had told us that Verulia needed the money from all those tickets that people were going to buy to see the exhibit. If Slouch stole the treasures, there wouldn't be anything *to* exhibit. Thinking about it all was giving me a stomachache.

"You look pretty glum."

It was Fox. I had slunk into one of the orange plastic chairs bolted to the floor and now he sat across from me. I said, "I guess I don't see a lot to be thrilled about."

"I think your flying is pretty cool."

"You do?"

"Who wouldn't? It's awesome."

"You don't think I'm, like, a freak?"

"Different, sure. But not a freak."

"Thanks. You know the other day, when you asked me to have a whipped caramel-chocolatino drink with you?"

"I guess now I know why you turned me down. My dad was trying to catch you."

"I felt really awful about it."

"You did? That's good, isn't it? Listen, I know my dad seems really odd. He's just got this thing about catching mythical creatures. Because of what happened to him when he was a kid."

"What do you mean?"

"When my dad was little, his parents took him on a camping trip. One day he wandered off and couldn't find his way home through the woods. He got really scared. He came to this lake and he sat down and started to cry. And then he heard a voice."

"A voice?"

"Really, it was more like singing. He looked at the water and saw a woman swimming there. But the woman had a tail, like a fish."

"You mean a mermaid?"

"I guess so. She asked my dad what was wrong and he told her. She told him not to worry, and then she started to sing again, in a beautiful voice. Her singing attracted the attention of my dad's parents, who were looking for him. They came rushing past the edge of the woods and picked my dad up in their arms. When he told them what happened, they all turned to the water, but there was nobody there. They said he must have fallen asleep and dreamed it, but my dad says it really happened. I guess he's been trying to find mythical creatures ever since, to prove it. I think he made a wrong turn somewhere in his thinking, you know. It's like he got lost."

"Yeah, I do know," I said, thinking of my own dad and how he'd been out of work. It seemed that I wasn't the only person with parent troubles – or rather, troubled parents.

"Anyway," Fox said, "I'm going to get us out of here."

"You are?"

"You bet."

Maybe Fox thought it was his job to look brave and rescue me. He really had no idea of what Solly and I had gone through facing Kaspar Snit in the last couple of years. I said, "We have to be careful. Slouch is more dangerous than he looks. He only cares about himself. I wouldn't rush into anything."

"I can manage him," Fox said, looking determined. Then he got up and walked over to the counter. He put his hands on it and called out to Slouch, who was taking a long drink from a giant slushie.

"Ah, excuse me, Mr. Slouch."

"What is it? I'm busy."

"Yes, I see that. But I think we should talk about all this. I'm sure we can come up with a reasonable solution to this little dilemma we're in."

Slouch put down the slushie and came up to the counter, rubbing his bald head and smiling. "Do you? That's very reasonable of you. Tell me, have you got any money on you?"

"I think so," Fox said. "Let me check." He reached into his jean pocket and pulled out a five-dollar bill. "I think I've got some change too." He felt around in his other pocket and came up with some coins. "Let me see. Seventy-five, eighty – ninety-three cents. That's five dollars and ninety-three cents."

"And you wouldn't mind handing it over? You'd do that for the sake of the others?" Slouch said, nodding in my direction.

"Sure I would."

"That's fine."

Slouch held out his hand and Fox placed the money

138

onto his palm. Slouch smiled and put it into his own pocket.

"Boy, are you easy to con."

"Con?"

"Now go back and sit with your flying friend over there. Go on, shoo."

Fox turned around and walked back, his determined look now gone from his face. In fact, his head was drooping in defeat as he dropped into the chair.

"Don't feel bad," I said. "It was your first time."

"All right, everyone," Slouch bellowed, from behind the counter. "Enough socializing. This isn't a tea party, you know. We've got a little job to do, so snap to it. I need Solly, Levon du Plessy-Minsk and his son, and Mr. Mustache. Back in the kitchen with me."

"What about Eleanor?" Solly said.

"Oh, I've got something special lined up for her. Now come on, step up here and stand in a circle."

As they came over the counter, Slouch directed them to a raised, shiny-metal platform like a disk, only with holes in it and a pole up the center. "The four of you, get up here, backs to the pole."

"What if we simply refuse?" Kaspar Snit asked.

"*Hmm*, let's see. I could ask you nicely. Pretty please? I could start to cry. Or I could make something bad happen to your friend Eleanor. You wouldn't want that, would you? No, I didn't think so. Cooperate like little lambs and everybody will be safe. It's as simple as that. Isn't this fun?"

All four of them were now standing on the metal platform in a circle around the pole, looking puzzled. "Is this some kind of time-travel portal?" Solly asked.

"You think you're in a science fiction movie? Get real, kid. Now stay still. For your own safety."

Slouch picked up a long rope and began to wind it tightly around them. He pulled it across their shoulders, then their waists, and then their ankles, before tying it with three knots. When he was sure they couldn't move, he rubbed his hands together. "Those years in the Boy Scouts sure paid off."

"Maybe we're safe," said Kaspar Snit, "but what about Eleanor?"

"Safe?" Slouch said. "Did I say you would be safe if you let me tie you up? What a slip of the tongue. What I meant to say was, you would be sorry."

"What exactly do you mean?" Levon du Plessy-Minsk asked.

"It's very simple. You're standing on the lid of the patented Rooster's chicken chunk fryer. Maybe I can't create inventions like Snitty over there, but I can borrow one, can't I? Right beneath you, under the metal platform you're standing on, is a cauldron of boiling oil."

The four of them looked down at their feet. I looked too. Now I understood! The platform would be covered in chicken chunks and then lowered into the cauldron below. The hot oil would come up through the holes. *Solly and the others would be deep-fried!*

Solly looked scared, but he said, "I hope there's no trans fat in that oil. I'm trying to stay healthy."

"That's very good," Kaspar Snit said. "I wish I could tell a joke like that."

"Really, Kaspar, it just takes practise."

"Would you two shut up? Neither of you will be telling jokes if Eleanor doesn't cooperate with me. I'm setting the timer here for exactly one hour from now. That should be just enough time for us to perform the little task that I've got planned. And *if* we get back in time, we can turn the timer off. But if not? Well, the four of you are going to be made into giant-sized fast food. Don't you just love it?"

"Love it?" Solly said. "I don't even like chicken chunks."

"What do I have to do?" Eleanor said.

"Oh, nothing difficult. You just have to be your charming self, that's all, and sweet-talk your old friend the ambassador into letting us into the exhibit early." From his pocket he pulled the minivan keys. "Now don't worry. We'll lock the door behind us."

Slouch signaled to me with a crooked finger to follow.

A FREE
GUIDED
TOUR

Slouch unlocked the door of the restaurant with a key and let us out before locking it again. Without being able to look through a window, I'd almost forgotten that it wasn't yet night. He marched us over to the minivan and unlocked the side door. "Go on, get in," he said. "You don't want us to waste any time, do you?"

I hesitated a moment, then got in. "Now that's the right attitude. Put on your seat belt. I wouldn't want anything to happen to you. Constance Foote Museum of Art, here we come."

Slouch turned the key. The minivan coughed, roared, sputtered, and died. "What a piece of junk," he muttered. "Come on, come on. . . ."

"Mr. du Plessy-Minsk did say it was temperamental."

"Listen, there isn't a car on this polluted planet that I can't drive. There we go, it started. I've got the touch. Now let's move."

Slouch put his foot on the gas and sped out of the parking lot onto the road. He wasn't a very good driver – the minivan kept weaving back and forth. I held on to the seat.

"Slouch," I said. "Being an evil genius didn't make Kaspar Snit happy. Why do you think that you'll be any different?"

"You're not getting it, Eleanor. I'm not like your buddy Kaspar Snit used to be. He enjoyed those fiendish plans of his. The more devious the better. He liked the attention, the fame. I don't have such a grand sense of myself. I'm just a little guy who wants to live the good life. If I could invent a shampoo that grew hair on bald heads, I'd do that. If I could write a best-selling book about a bunch of orphans and a count who wants their inheritance, I'd do that. But the problem is, I can't. Sure, I had thought that working for Kaspar Snit was going to be the answer. Houses, swimming pools, private jets – the works. But I was wrong. He turned out to be a loser and, even worse, a softy. Instead of getting out of jail and coming up with a better plan to take advantage of people, what does he do? He goes all gooey-hearted and wants to go straight. So now I've got to get rich on my own. Don't bother giving me one of your Goody Two-shoes speeches. Kaspar Snit turned out to have a weak spot in his heart, a little place that got infected by the goodness germ. But you know what I've got in here?" he said, thumping his chest and swerving even more. "I've got a heart-shaped piggy bank. All it wants is to hear the clink of cash. You got that, kiddo?"

"I've got it," I muttered.

"Good. Because here we are, the place that's going to make my little dreamy-dreams come true."

Slouch swerved the minivan towards the curb, bumping it with his front tire, and thumped to a stop. I looked out the window and saw the marble columns that marked the entrance of the Constance Foote Museum of Art. I could see a banner announcing the exhibit hanging between the columns. Some workers in gray overalls were carrying in wooden crates, while a museum guard held open the big front door.

"Do we go in?" I asked, anxious about the timer ticking away.

"Hold your horses. I have to look the part. Where's that knapsack? Ah, here, in the back. Let's see. . . ."

Slouch fished in the knapsack and pulled out his black wig. He stuck it on his bald head and, looking in the mirror, adjusted it. Then he took out the fake mustache and stuck it over his lip. He adjusted the ends to make the curl on either side match.

"May I introduce myself?" he said, deepening his voice. "I am the evil genius Kaspar Snit."

He didn't look identical – his face was too round, his eyes too small – but he was close enough. "I do love field trips to the museum," he said. "But don't get lost. Just follow my lead. Remember, the lives of your whiny brother and the others are at stake. Now look happy, happy, happy."

Slouch left the minivan and I followed, walking beside him up the museum steps. He was shorter than Kaspar Snit and had a sideways waddle, but I wasn't sure if anyone would notice. We reached the top of the stairs, where a guard in uniform stood before the tall doors.

"If you don't mind getting out of the way," said Slouch.

"I do mind, sir. The museum is closed until Friday. Big new exhibit going in."

"Yes, I know. That's exactly why we're here. Now we'll just –"

The guard put his hand on the door. "No, you will not, sir. There are valuable items in there and the new security system is still being installed. No unauthorized visitors allowed."

"But we are authorized, you see."

"By whom, may I ask?"

"By the ambassador from Verulia. He is a personal friend of this young girl. And an old acquaintance of mine, you might say. In fact, I used to be his employer."

The guard looked at me and then Slouch. It was true that the ambassador had been in Kaspar Snit's warrior army, but that wasn't exactly a job that he would remember fondly. Anyway, the guard didn't look like he believed Slouch and we might have been turned away again if the door hadn't been pushed open from the inside. Out stepped the ambassador himself, His Excellency H. Waldorf Mansfield. He wore a dark suit with the crest of Verulia on it and would have looked pretty sharp if there hadn't been plaster dust all over him.

"Did I hear a problem out here?" the ambassador asked. He looked at me and smiled. "Why, if it isn't Eleanor Blande! A true friend of Verulia. How good to see you. But who is this you're with? May I introduce my . . . my . . . oh my, oh my!"

His Excellency's eyes had moved from me to Kaspar Snit – or rather, to Slouch in disguise. "Yes, my good man," Slouch said, trying to lower his voice, "it's me, Kaspar Snit. Your old friend."

"Friend? You were hardly a friend. You forced me into your terrible army, treated us all like slaves, and wouldn't let me dance."

"Must you be so picky? Anyway, I am a different person now. I've reformed and am leading an ordinary life. Isn't that right, Eleanor?"

The ambassador looked to me for an answer. How I wanted to tell him the truth – that Kaspar Snit had reformed, but that this wasn't him. But I said, "Yes, Wally, that's right. He's a friend of the family now."

"I'd heard something about this," the ambassador said. "And I am most gratified by it. Mr. Snit, let me shake your hand. My, but you do feel clammy. And you seem a little different. Have you shrunk?"

"I used to wear platform heels."

"Your voice is a little odd as well."

"I've been taking singing lessons."

"Well, I'd love to stay and chat, but I've got so much to do. Here, Mr. Snit," he said, pulling a square card out of his jacket pocket, "have an invitation to the opening on Friday."

"Oh, dear," said Slouch. "I'd love to go, but I have to leave town on Thursday. To see my sick aunt. You don't suppose that you could let Eleanor and me in for a quick peek, do you?"

"Well, I don't know," the ambassador said, hesitantly.

"Just for old time's sake?"

"All right. I'll give you a quick tour. There are so many priceless objects. I wouldn't want you to miss them. Come inside, then."

"You are too kind. Lead the way."

The guard held the door for us and we followed the ambassador into the great hall. He took us past the ticket booth to an enormous stone archway that was the entrance to the exhibit. Inside, workers in yellow hard hats were hammering nails, lifting up signs, and moving boxes around. A man in a white hard hat came up to the ambassador.

"Everything's on schedule, Your Excellency."

"That's wonderful news."

"I was just about to call a break."

"Good timing. It will give me the chance to show my friends around."

The workman blew his whistle and we waited for the men and women to file out of the exhibition hall. All around us, gold and silver objects glittered in their glass cases and from special stands. "These silver goblets were once used by the ancient kings of Verulia," the ambassador said, leading us to a cabinet. "And over here are necklaces and rings from the royal court. Most of these objects have been stored away for years. With the money from the ticket sales, we're going to build a splendid new museum of our own, where schoolchildren will come on field trips and learn about their heritage. They'll see how we moved from war to peace, from creating weapons to creating art."

"It's all so beautiful," I said. "But what's supposed to be here?"

I was looking at a slim glass stand with a velvet background. A small spotlight shone on the stand, but there was nothing on it.

"I see what you're staring at – the missing amulet."

"The *what?*"

The ambassador said, "Back in 1901, a trove of precious objects was found in an ancient cave in the Verulian mountains. For many years it was left there, and travelers who were adventurous enough to go so far would enter the cave to see it. But, one day, an artifact was discovered missing – a small silver amulet that had belonged to a Verulian princess. A terrible shame, for it was of great historical significance. All we have left is a very old photograph, taken with an early camera. The photo's against the wall. It hasn't been hung yet."

The ambassador lifted the photograph, which had been blown up large and mounted on a board. It was grainy and spotted, but I could see the amulet – a crooked rectangle with the raised design of a quarter moon and three stars. It was the very same amulet that had given my mother the power of flying! That I had pressed into my own hand and that had left a permanent mark on my palm.

But the amulet had been lost when the pigeon in Misery Mountain had flown off with it. What a shame that we couldn't give it back to Verulia. *How had it come into my family's possession in the first place?* I remembered what my mother had told me, that my great-great-grandmother had found it during her travels to the Middle East. She must have traveled to Verulia too. *Had she really found the amulet, or had she been the one who had swiped it?*

"Fascinating, I'm sure," said Slouch, "but wouldn't it be more interesting to look at objects that are actually here? For example, what is this long golden box shaped like a person standing here? Those can't be real rubies and sapphires and diamonds all over it."

"Indeed, they are. Exactly one thousand precious jewels. In fact, this is the most valuable object in the collection by far, the sarcophagus of the last king of Verulia."

"That's some fancy coffin," Slouch said. "Why isn't it in a case?"

"We're going to put an electrical security field around it."

"So if a person had that sarcophagus, and sold the jewels, he'd be stinking rich," Slouch said.

"The richest man on earth, I'd expect. Of course, it would be criminal to ruin it by removing them."

"Well, it's a good thing I'm a criminal. Eleanor, I think we've found what we want."

"I beg your pardon?" the ambassador said.

"You heard me. We'll use that dolly with the big wheels over there. Help us get it out of the museum and into our minivan."

"Of course I won't help you. Do you mean you're not really reformed? You're still an evil genius!"

"Bingo!" Slouch smiled. "That's right, me, Kaspar Snit, capital *K*, capital *S*, is about to steal the great sarcophagus of Verulia. And you're going to let us. You know why? Because if you don't, something very nasty is going to happen to Eleanor's brother, Solly, and a few other people for good measure. You wouldn't want that to happen, would you?"

The ambassador looked at me. "Eleanor, is this true?"

"I'm sorry, Wally. It is true. And we've got to hurry if we want to save Solly."

"Then I've got no choice. This is terrible, tragic. What will the people of Verulia say? Their prize possession gone! It will be a scandal."

"Yeah, yeah, save the sob story for later. Now help lift this thing. It's even heavier than it looks."

"You will pay for this, Kaspar Snit," said the ambassador.

"You think so? Well, when you catch Kaspar Snit – I mean me, of course – make sure you put him – I mean me – in jail for a long, long time. Now let's go."

The sarcophagus really was heavy. But we wrestled it onto the dolly, and Slouch and the ambassador grabbed the handles and wheeled it out of the exhibit hall. We went through the front doors, where the ambassador nodded to the guards, and then down a ramp at the side of the stairs to the waiting minivan. Slouch opened the back doors, put down the metal ramp, and the two of them pushed it up and in.

Slouch slammed the doors shut. "Thanks, Wally," he said. "You've been a real help. You better stand back if you don't want me to accidentally back up onto your foot."

A moment later, we were in the seats and Slouch was starting the engine.

"Ha! Who's the baddest baddy around now?"

"You are," I said. And meant it.

A SHOCK
TO THE
SYSTEM

In the car, Slouch looked at his watch. "Nineteen minutes exactly," he said. "That might just be enough time. Wait a minute, I almost forgot. I need Kaspar Snit alive. After all, he's the one they'll think is the thief. I better step on it."

He couldn't have remembered before? Now Slouch turned the key in the ignition. The engine burbled, hiccuped, and went dead. He banged on the dashboard. "Come on, start!" Again he turned the key. Two coughs, a roar, a stutter, and then . . . nothing. "Why, I'll send you to the junk heap if you don't get moving!" Now he turned the key hard and put his foot on the gas, making the minivan roar and die.

"I think you flooded the engine," I said. "My dad told me about that. Now you have to wait a minute. And we need that minute to get back in time!"

"Stop whining. Let me try again. See, I'll be gentle as a lamb."

Slouch put two fingers daintily on the key and slowly turned it. The engine coughed, burped, and started. "Hold on to your hat!" he said, as he hit the gas. We went speeding forward. Whenever we hit a pothole, the sarcophagus bumped against the walls of the minivan. It was only then that I had a chance to consider the fact that it had been made for a dead person to lie in. *Was there a mummified body in it now – an ancient, moldy king?* Maybe there was a curse on anyone who stole it, like in old horror movies. If so, I hoped that it could tell the difference between me and Slouch.

Through the side window, I watched buildings speed by. When I turned to look out the front, I saw us barreling towards a red light.

"STOP!"

Slouch hit the brake. We screeched to a halt just before a truck passed in front of us. *That was close!* But from the back of the minivan, I heard a bang, crash, and thump.

"What the heck was that?" Slouch asked.

I turned around. "It's the sarcophagus! You didn't lock the back doors."

The sudden stop must have caused the heavy sarcophagus to bang against the doors, swing them open, and drop out. Slouch and I looked at each other and screamed at the same time. In a flash, we were out of the minivan and scrambling behind. There was the sarcophagus, lying on the road!

"How much time do we have?" I asked.

"Twelve minutes. We have to lift this thing together. Ready? One, two, *three!*"

Man, was it heavy. But Slouch and I managed to tilt up the end and slide it back into the van. We threw the doors closed again and Slouch made sure they were locked.

In front of us, the light had turned green. Cars began honking behind us. We ran back, jumped into our seats, and Slouch hit the gas before I even had my door closed. Now he hunched over the wheel, muttering under his breath as he drove as fast as he could. When Rooster's Fried Chicken came into view, I asked, "How much time now?"

"Six minutes!"

The minivan shot into the parking lot and rattled up to the door. I practically threw myself out onto the ground.

"Wait!" Slouch said. "I'm not leaving the sarcophagus in the van. It's my winning lottery ticket. Help me bring it in."

"But hurry!" I pleaded. Slouch opened the back doors and we both jumped up. I helped him get the sarcophagus onto the dolly and we wheeled it down the ramp. Then Slouch unlocked the restaurant door and we pushed it inside.

"Eleanor, is that you?" Solly cried from the kitchen. "Hurry up! The timer's got two minutes and forty seconds to go!"

Even Slouch's eyes widened. We ran to the counter and climbed over it, Slouch tumbling to the floor on the other side. He got up again and hurried over to the timer.

154

"It's stuck," he said. "Too much chicken grease. It won't turn off."

"We have to untie the ropes!" I cried. Quickly I climbed onto the platform and started working at the knot behind Kaspar Snit's hands. "You did too good a job," I said to Slouch. "I can't undo it. Get a knife."

"Hey, who are you to give orders? I'll order myself to get a knife. But I don't want to be on that platform in case it starts to go down. Here, you do it."

Slouch held the knife up. I grabbed it and started sawing away.

"I tried to get G.W. to gnaw it with his teeth," Solly said. "But I guess I forgot to teach him that command."

"Look at the timer!" called Levon du Plessy-Minsk. "There's less than fifty seconds!"

"Please calm yourself," said Kaspar Snit. "Eleanor is doing the best she can."

I was more than halfway through, then three-quarters. One more strand to go . . . and it was cut through! The rope fell away and everyone shook themselves out of it and jumped off the platform.

"Eleanor, get off!" Fox shouted. But somehow I couldn't get myself to move. My arms and legs felt frozen. Kaspar Snit was the only one tall enough; he reached up and put his hands around my waist. A second later, the platform dropped from under me and I looked down to see the oil bubbling up through the holes.

Kaspar Snit put me down. "Thanks," I said.

"No, we all must thank you," Kaspar Snit said.

"Hey, why doesn't somebody thank me?" Slouch said. "Better yet, why don't you all shut up! It's the top of the hour. I want to check the TV news report."

From under the counter, Slouch pulled out a small television set. He pulled up the bunny ears and turned it on. The screen crackled to life, although the black-and-white picture was fuzzy. I could see the puffy-haired female reporter standing outside the Constance Foote Museum of Art, talking to Officer Yogis, who held his cap in his hands.

– And do you have any idea who committed this theft?

– As a matter of fact, we do. Our prime suspect is Kaspar Snit, former fountain thief and robber of little children. This looks like his work. In fact, we have an eyewitness description. We are also looking for a thirteen-year-old girl named Eleanor Blande.

– Is this thirteen-year-old girl considered dangerous?

– Well, I wouldn't go that far.

– Thank you, Officer. You heard it here first, ladies and gentlemen. Kaspar Snit and his dangerous accomplice, Eleanor Blande, are on the loose. In the meantime, the opening of the State Treasures of Verulia exhibit has been indefinitely postponed due to the theft of the exhibit's priceless sarcophagus. Stay tuned to this channel for any developments.

Slouch snapped off the television. "It worked!" he said, hopping about with glee. "It worked, it worked! They think that Kaspar Snit is the thief! They'll never catch me. I'm rich and I'm happy. Oh, yes!"

Slouch danced about, right up to the sarcophagus. He pretended to bow to it and kiss an imaginary hand. "Ah, dear dead king, how delightful to see you," he said. "All those diamonds and rubies and sapphires and pearls that you are wearing! It's such a shame that I have to take them."

Fox looked at me. "Is he talking to a *coffin*?" he said.

"Not just any old coffin," Slouch said. "Now, where's that knife, Eleanor? I can use it to pry these jewels off. Let's start with this diamond. *Hmm,* it's stuck, but if I just . . ."

As he was touching the tip of the knife to the sarcophagus, Slouch stopped. We all knew why.

There was a sound coming from inside it. A low moaning.

"What's that? Is someone playing a trick on me? It's not funny, Solly."

"I didn't do anything," Solly said.

We all looked at the sarcophagus. The moaning began again and it was definitely coming from inside. The sarcophagus was shaking too.

We all jumped back.

The moaning grew louder.

"What *is* that?" Slouch asked, in a trembling voice. "It can't be. I don't believe in curses. Please, whatever you are, don't come and get me. That girl stole you, not me. It was her!"

"What a coward," Fox said.

Kaspar Snit stepped forward. "There's only one way to find out what's in there." He cleared his throat and announced in his most commanding voice, "Whatever you are, we are going to release you. We ask that you cause us no harm." He reached forward and grabbed the edge of the lid. Planting his feet firmly, he gritted his teeth and pulled.

Slowly the lid began to open. A wave of dust spilled out, clouding the air. I could hear something inside. Coughing. And then a voice.

"Thank goodness, I could hardly breathe. Children, it is good to see you again."

"Mrs. Leer!" Solly cried. He ran and hugged her, even as she was stepping out.

"Solly, dearest boy," she said, hugging him back. "But I'm getting you all covered in this old dust. And Eleanor! Come here, my darling."

I couldn't believe it! I ran and hugged Mrs. Leer too. When I turned around again, I saw that Kaspar Snit's face had turned pale.

"Mrs. Leer," he said. "It is a surprise, I must say, a great surprise to see you in such a situation."

"You mean, stuck in a coffin, Mr. Snit? A good thing it had a couple of holes in the back, or I would have run out of air."

"I knew there was no curse," Slouch said. "I was just pretending to be scared. But what were you doing there in the first place? You don't exactly figure into my plans."

"I happened to have been visiting the ambassador at the

museum. Your parents, dear children, telephoned me as soon as they realized you were missing. They've been frantically looking for you. Naturally, I came right away. I thought the ambassador might know something, so I went to see him. When I saw Kaspar Snit enter the hall, I quickly decided to hide. Of course, I heard everything and thought that I had better come along for the ride. I knew that way I would find you."

"And you did find us!" Solly said.

Kaspar Snit stepped forward. "And you found me in the same situation, Mrs. Leer. You view my lowly position for yourself."

"I do, Mr. Snit, and it is a shock, sir, a shock to the system. And yet I must say that it gladdens my heart to discover that you are not behind this brazen act."

"Please, call me Kaspar."

"If that disagreeable man will just let us go," Mrs. Leer said, "I'm sure the authorities will be more lenient with him."

"Oh, sure, I'll let you go," Slouch said. "And I'll give you a tuna fish sandwich and a glass of milk in case you get hungry."

"Have you got chocolate milk?" said Solly.

"I'm being sarcastic. Nobody is going nowhere."

"That is a double negative," said Mrs. Leer. "It means we are, in fact, going somewhere."

"Well spotted," said Kaspar Snit. "I see that you, too, are a lover of proper language."

"Indeed, I am. It is my second love, next to Irish music."

"I regret that, as a child, I had no interest in the piano lessons that my mother made me take," Kaspar Snit said. "I was interested only in tormenting the piano teacher."

"It is not too late to learn, Mr. Snit. For example, you might take up the Bodhran, the Irish drum."

"I do wish you would call me Kaspar."

"Excuse me for interrupting this adorable conversation," Slouch said. "But it's time to say good-bye to our friend Mr. Kaspar Snit. Because you, boss, are free to go."

"I am?" said Kaspar Snit.

"Yessiree."

"Good. Because I plan to go straight to the police."

"I should hope so," Slouch said.

"You do?"

"Yes. You're going to go to the police and confess that you did it."

"But why on earth would I do that?"

"Because I'll still be holding the rest of these suckers. And I'm not going to let them go until you tell the police that you stole the sarcophagus. Then, even if Eleanor tells them you didn't, they won't believe her. Meanwhile, I'll be on my brand-new yacht somewhere on the Riviera, drinking champagne. Got it, boss?"

"Yes, I've got it," Kaspar Snit said darkly.

"Good. Now you can go. We're going to turn on the television in exactly half an hour and we expect to see a report of your capture."

Kaspar Snit brushed off his cape. "I am ready."

"But you can't do it!" I said to Kaspar. "You can't go to jail again, not when you didn't do anything."

"Please, Eleanor, do not interfere. I know what I must do." Kaspar Snit moved towards the door. Slouch followed him and unlocked it. Kaspar Snit hesitated a moment, then turned back to us. "Farewell, Lucretia," he said, swooping into a deep bow. "If I might just leave you with this . . ."

From a pocket inside his cape, Kaspar Snit drew a folded piece of paper.

"What is it?" Mrs. Leer said, taking the paper.

"A poem."

A moment later, he was gone through the door. Slouch was locking it again.

"I have absolutely no idea," Levon du Plessy-Minsk said, "what is going on."

A DEN OF
THIEVES

After Kaspar was gone, Slouch announced that the thought of his new fortune was making him hungry. But nobody else wanted a chicken-on-a-stick, so he went into the kitchen to eat one by himself.

With Slouch busy, Solly and I had a chance to catch up with Mrs. Leer. First, we introduced her to Levon du Plessy-Minsk.

"You're a what?" she asked.

"A creature catcher," Levon du Plessy-Minsk said. "Actually, a former creature catcher. I'd rather not go into it."

"And this is Fox, Mrs. Leer."

"Hi," Fox said, holding out his hand.

Mrs. Leer shook it. "The pleasure is mine." She turned to me and, in a loud voice, said, "He's a nice-looking boy. A little skinny, maybe. And he could use a haircut. He reminds me of youthful pictures of the dear, dreary Mr. Leer, except of course Mr. Leer was bowlegged and had a much larger nose."

"We can't believe you're here," I said, anxious to change the subject.

"I can hardly believe it myself. Just yesterday, I was taking care of six children in Budapest," she said. "The most spoiled bunch you can imagine. Had their own giraffe as a pet. But I got them in shape soon enough. Then your parents called me and I hopped on the first plane. Of course, they'd already been to the police. Naturally they assumed that you were kidnapped by Kaspar Snit. They're very angry at themselves for giving you permission to spend time with him."

"But it wasn't him," Solly said.

"I'm sure they'll be glad to hear that, if we can get out of here. And how is my favorite big-eared, long-toothed fellow with the beady eyes?"

"I'm okay," Solly said.

"I didn't mean you, I meant G.W."

"Oh, he's fine. He's in my backpack, see? Only he's sick of chicken chunks."

"I can't say I blame him. So there's no way out of here, eh? Everything's locked up, is it?"

"I'm afraid so," I said.

"And what about your flying powers, dear? This is just the sort of thing they ought to be good for."

"Nowhere to fly out of."

"That's a pity."

Just then, Slouch came bouncing over the counter. "It's the top of the hour; the news is going to be on," he said. "Time to turn on the TV."

I watched as the screen crackled to life again. First there was a Tuxedo Toothpaste commercial (*"Take your teeth out for a night on the town!"*). And then the symbol for the news and then the reporter with the puffy hair standing in front of the police station. She held out her microphone as Officer Yogis led two other police officers with a hold on Kaspar Snit. Kaspar Snit wasn't struggling, but the officers were holding him tightly anyway, leading him towards a waiting police car.

– Ladies and gentleman, I am standing outside the local police precinct just as the recently captured suspect in the Verulian sarcophagus heist is being led away. And it is none other than Kaspar Snit, well-known to police for his previous ingenious evil deeds. Officer Yogis, did he put up a struggle?

– Not at all. He was quiet as a mouse. In fact, he gave himself up.

– Do you consider him highly dangerous?

— It's always wise to be careful.

— Ah, here's Kaspar Snit! Mr. Snit, do you have an alibi for the crime?

— No.

— Then how do you plan to defend yourself?

— I don't plan to defend myself. I did it. I stole the sarcophagus.

— Did you hear that, viewers? Kaspar Snit has just made a confession on national television! You heard it here first! Now stay tuned for the regional handball scores.

Slouch snapped off the TV, pulled himself up onto the counter, and started moonwalking backwards. "Oh, yeah, who's *the man*? I am, that's who. Slouch rules!"

He fell off the counter.

"Mr. Slouch," said Mrs. Leer, as he got up again, "you are a very bad man."

"Also a very bad dancer," said Solly.

Levon du Plessy-Minsk came forward. "Now that you have everything you want, you can let us go, right?"

"Almost right," said Slouch. "I need just one more thing. I have to sell the jewels on the sarcophagus. It's money I want, not glitter. As soon as I have my money, you can all go free."

"All right," said Fox, "so how are you going to sell stolen jewels, anyway?"

At that Slouch stood still. He looked at Fox. He looked at me. He looked at Mrs. Leer. Then he started banging the top of his head with the flat of his hand.

"Stupid Slouch! Stupid, stupid, stupid!"

"What are you doing?" I said.

Slouch stopped banging his head. "I forgot to figure out how I'm going to sell the jewels."

"You've got to be kidding."

"There's been a lot to think about, you know. I've been under a lot of pressure. Being an evil genius is a big responsibility. When I was Kaspar Snit's assistant, I only had to do what I was told. I didn't have to figure it all out myself."

"Geez," Solly said. "Maybe you should have stayed a sidekick. I just don't think you're evil-genius material."

"That hurts, you know," Slouch said. "It's not as if I don't have feelings."

Just then came a knock on the door.

We all turned and stared at the locked door. The knock came again, only louder. Slouch frowned and stepped towards the door.

"We're closed for renovations," he shouted. "Try Priscilla's Pancake Emporium down the highway."

"We're not coming for food," said a voice. It had a heavy accent, but I couldn't tell from what country. "We are coming to buy jewels."

"Jewels?"

"Yes. Valuable jewels," said a woman's voice, also with an accent.

"Preferably stolen," said the man.

"We have cash," said the woman.

Slouch turned and grinned at us, holding out his palms. "Hear that, do you? Who looks stupid now? It's just like they say: If you have a product that people want, they come knocking at your door." He took out his key and unlocked the door. In came two odd-looking people, with silk scarves over their mouths. The woman wore a fake fur coat over a polka-dot dress and high heels. The man wore a very old pin-striped suit, which was too small for him, and white tennis sneakers. Each of them carried a small suitcase.

"Hey, what's with the scarves?" Slouch said.

"We must protect our identities," said the man. "How do we know it is even safe here? You are a den of thieves."

"Actually," Solly said, "we're more like a fast-food restaurant of thieves."

"Do you really have cash?" Slouch asked.

"We do," said the man, tapping on his suitcase.

"Let me see it," Slouch said.

"All right," said the woman, "but do not get too close."

She and the man bent down to unlatch their suitcases. They opened the lids just enough for us to see the thick piles of bills inside. "You have the jewels?" said the man.

"Right over there. But they're still on the sarcophagus. I can just pry them off."

"No need. We will take it like that. But first, we need to examine it. Does it open?"

"Why?" Slouch said. "Do you want to use it for your socks and underwear?"

"We don't like smart talk," said the man. "If you are not careful, we will buy our jewels somewhere else."

"I'm sorry. Please, go ahead and open it. There's no extra charge for the dust."

The man pulled open the lid, causing another cloud to rise. He stepped forward and then, to my surprise, tried to step into it. But he seemed to have trouble fitting in his elbows.

"It is no good. A person doesn't fit."

"You want a person to fit in it?"

"For sleeping, of course."

"Well, if you want to sleep inside a coffin, that's your business. But I assure you that a person can fit in it. Move aside, I'll show you. It's just the way you're holding your arms. Watch. . . ."

Slouch pushed the man aside and stepped backwards into the sarcophagus. He put his knees together and crossed his arms so that he fit snugly inside. There was a smudge of dust across his bald head.

"See?" he said. "I fit perfectly."

"Yes, you do," said the woman. "That's very good. And now we will see if the lid can shut."

At that moment, she and the man pushed the lid shut.

"Hey, what are you doing?" came Slouch's muffled voice. "It's dark in here!"

The man pulled off the scarf covering his face. "Hello, everybody."

"Dad!" I cried.

"Don't forget me," the woman said, pulling off hers.

"Mom!"

"Who were you expecting?" Dad said. "Laurel and Hardy?"

Kaspar Snit had told the police just what Slouch had wanted him to. But when Mom and Dad came to visit Kaspar in jail, he felt that he had to tell them where Solly and I were. My parents had come to rescue us on their own.

Officer Yogis did finally arrive, along with a squad car of other police officers, when my dad telephoned from the booth outside to say that they had found the sarcophagus *and* the thief.

"A nice little package," Officer Yogis said, tapping on the lid of the sarcophagus. "Knock, knock."

"Who's there?" answered Slouch from inside.

"Robin."

"Robin who?"

"Robin de museum was a very naughty thing to do."

Then he had two officers open it up and haul Slouch out. "Please arrest me," Slouch said. "I don't want to hear any more jokes."

"Better call ahead to the station," Officer Yogis told one of the policemen. "They can release Kaspar Snit. We need the room."

Mom, Dad, Solly, me, Levon du Plessy-Minsk, Fox, and Mrs. Leer all watched as the police cars pulled out of the Rooster's Fried Chicken parking lot. "Slouch should never have tried to be an evil genius," Dad said. "He wasn't cut out for it."

"Yeah," Solly said, "but you have to admire the ambition."

Solly and I were sure glad to get home. Now that we were free, boy, were we starving. We would have eaten just about anything, except for chicken. Mrs. Leer came to stay with us, and we all helped in the kitchen. Mom and Dad put about everything there was in the fridge on the table and we ate until we were stuffed.

Just as we were finishing, the doorbell rang. "I'll get it," I said, but Solly got up too and we both raced for the door, trying to get there first. It was a tie. We struggled to open it, finally pulling the door open together. There stood Kaspar Snit.

Black cape. Shiny hair. Mustache curled. Holding . . . a rose.

"*Ahem,*" he said, clearing his throat. "Good evening, Eleanor, Solly."

"Kaspar, you're all scrubbed up," said Solly. "And that's a brand-new cape."

"Is it? Well, perhaps. I hope I'm not disturbing your supper."

"We are just going to have dessert. Come on in," I said, pulling his arm.

Solly and I accompanied Kaspar Snit to the dining room. "Ah, I am interrupting," he said, as soon as he saw

Mom, Dad, and Mrs. Leer at the table. "I can come back another time."

"No, please join us for dessert," Mom said, getting up. "We've an empty seat right here. I'll get you a plate."

"That is most kind of you."

"Is that rose for me?" Dad said. Kaspar Snit stared at him with such horror that Dad had to quickly say, "I was just kidding."

"Yes, of course you were," Kaspar Snit said, and then forced himself to laugh. It was the fakest laugh I'd ever heard. Boy, was he nervous. He came forward and held out the rose. "Mrs. Leer," he said. "A small token of my affection."

"How kind of you," she said, taking it. "The dear, dreary Mr. Leer was partial to giving me enormous bouquets of flowers."

Kaspar Snit looked defeated, but he sat down and Mom came back with a plate for him. Then Dad served us each a piece of Mrs. Leer's chocolate-chip pistachio Swiss-cheese pie.

"I am not overly partial to sweets," he said.

"It is my own recipe," Mrs. Leer said. "The dear, dreary Mr. Leer could never get enough of it."

Those words were sufficient to make Kaspar Snit pick up his fork. He stared at the pie, forked up a large gooey mound, and put it in his mouth. All of us watched him slowly chewing. It was a long moment before he could speak.

"I have never tasted anything like it."

"I am so glad," Mrs. Leer said, happily. "The dear, dreary Mr. Leer used to say the same thing."

"Mrs. Leer," said Kaspar Snit, "I know how fond you were of your late husband. I know that no one could ever replace him, least of all myself. But I hope, Mrs. Leer, that I might be looked upon not as a constant point of comparison to that shining example of the male species, but simply as myself. I fear, ma'am, that, otherwise, my case shall be hopeless."

Mrs. Leer looked down. We all waited for her to speak – all except Solly, who was happily shoveling forkfuls of pie into his mouth.

"Mr. Snit, I see that you are right. While the memory of the dear, dreary Mr. Leer shall always be precious to me, I must accept those memories as the past. It is necessary to live in the present. I now wish to do so. I thank you for being patient."

"It is I who must thank you, Mrs. Leer, for even entertaining thoughts of one whose history is so disgraceful as my own. Perhaps when you are finished your dessert, you might want to take a postprandial stroll with me."

"I have never heard anyone use that word before," Mrs. Leer said, "and it is one of my favorites. I would be delighted."

All of us accompanied them to the front door and watched as Kaspar Snit and Mrs. Leer moved past our lawn, where the fountain used to be. Suddenly Solly called out, "Wait!"

Kaspar Snit and Mrs. Leer stopped and turned around.

"Yes?" said Kaspar Snit.

"You only got through seven of the ten lessons. You're not finished our course yet."

"Let's see," Mom said. "Lesson eight was *Perform a heroic act*, wasn't it? Well, Kaspar Snit did pick you up, Eleanor, when the fryer was about to drop."

"That's true," I said.

"And what was lesson nine? *Sacrifice yourself for your friends*. Kaspar Snit went to jail, even though he was innocent, just to protect all of you. I'd say that was putting your friends first, wouldn't you?"

"Hey, you're right," Solly said.

"Well, nine out of ten lessons is pretty good," Mom said. "I think Kaspar has learned enough. Lucretia, Kaspar, have a nice walk. It *is* a lovely evening, isn't it?"

And then she shooed us in and closed the door.

STRANGE/ ORDINARY AND ORDINARY/STRANGE

Spring turned into summer and life grew strange and ordinary at the same time. Ordinary because Solly and I went to school, came home, had outings with our parents, did homework, and hung out with our friends. Fox and I took bike rides together, saw movies, and every once in a while, Solly would sing, "Fox and Eleanor sitting in a tree . . ." and I would have to slug him. We weren't kidnapped, we weren't the inspiration for a television show, and nobody tried to film us flying. But it was also strange because, for the opening of the State Treasures of Verulia exhibit, our whole family went with Kaspar Snit and Mrs. Leer. Strange because my teacher for the rest of the year continued to be Kaspar Snit. He tried to be a good teacher, but it wasn't easy for him. Once he got so frustrated that he grabbed his own mustache by the ends and pulled until he screamed.

It was strange because Mrs. Leer did not go away at the end of her week's holiday. Instead, she took a nanny position with a family two blocks from us. That way she could spend her free evenings and weekends with Kaspar Snit.

"They're such an adorable couple," Mom said.

Adorable? Kaspar Snit? Now *that* was strange. But what was most strange was that I got used to these changes. After a while, they didn't seem strange at all.

There was one other new thing. Dad got a job. He still didn't have any fountain work and when he finally decided to stop being depressed by it, he got a job as a waiter at the Rooster's Fried Chicken restaurant. Only it wasn't called that anymore. A woman named Penelope Liftwich bought it and turned it into Rooster's Vegetarian Café. Dad worked there at lunchtime, mostly as a waiter but sometimes as a cook too. He missed his fountain work, but he liked the new job better than not working at all.

One night, when Mom came into my room to say good night, I said, "Can I ask you a question?"

"Of course, love."

"It's about the amulet. Do you think my great-great-grandmother stole it from that cave in Verulia? Is that how it ended up in our family?"

Mom sighed. "Well, she did travel around the world. And while nobody liked to talk about it, she did sometimes take things that didn't belong to her."

"Great," I said. "My great-great-grandmother was a grave robber."

"I'm afraid so," Mom said. "But it was a long time ago."

"If we still had the amulet, I guess we would have to give it back, now that we know where it came from. I mean, it belongs to Verulia. Besides, we can fly without it now."

"You mean, *you* can fly without it. And we can fly because of you. But, yes, we would give it back. There's nothing we can do about that now, though. Good night, Eleanor."

The next morning I woke up when Solly jumped on my head. He didn't mean to land on my head, he was just trying to get me up. "Come on, Eleanor, wake up! Dad has something to tell us! Hurry!"

So I pushed him onto the floor, got out of bed, and ran to the kitchen with Solly right behind. Mom was making pancakes for breakfast. I could see that Dad was glowing with excitement.

"I got this E-mail last night," he said. "It's from our friend Wally. I think you'd all like to hear it." And he started to read.

Dear Manfred,

Hope you and your family are well and nobody has been kidnapped lately. Wanted to tell you that our *State Treasures of Verulia* show was a great hit and the country made oodles of money from ticket sales.

After much discussion, the parliament of Verulia has decided how to spend part of the money. To make the country more beautiful, it has decided to put a fountain in every town square. That means three thousand and twenty-one fountains. The first and most grand is to be in the square of our capital city.

I have been asked by parliament to urgently request that you take on the position of supervisor for this major project. No one else has the experience, the taste, or the expertise for such an undertaking. We expect the work to take at least ten years, during which we would like you and your family to make frequent visits to our country. Salary to be negotiated. Your reply is needed immediately.

Yours truly,
H. Waldorf Mansfield, ambassador

"Are you going to do it?" Solly asked.
"Am I going to do it? It's the job of my dreams. *Yippee!*"
Dad picked up Mom and twirled her around while Solly and I hooted and hollered. Dad was a fountain expert again.

The summer holidays arrived. We spent our time having picnics, playing baseball, and swimming at the community pool. We were going to take a real holiday in the last two weeks of August. The government of Verulia was sending a special aeroplane to pick us up and take us there, so that we could be the guests of honor at a ceremony unveiling the first new fountain, in the main square of the capital city. Solly, Mom, and I hadn't been to Verulia since being trapped in Kaspar Snit's fortress, and we were all pretty excited to be going back.

The day before we were leaving, Kaspar Snit knocked on our door. He had been relieved to finish teaching for the year and had even let the class have a party – with a cake, ice cream, and balloons. Now he was spending the summer holidays "recovering," as he put it.

"Eleanor," Kaspar Snit said, as he stood in the doorway, "would you mind asking your parents if you could all drop in at my house? Say, six o'clock?"

"Sure," I said. Of course, Solly and I had been over many times, but we hadn't had an invitation since that first dinner when he moved onto the street.

"You don't suppose it's a trick?" Dad said. "I mean, maybe he's calling us over to kidnap us, or brainwash us, or for some other nefarious purpose."

Mom rolled her eyes. "Really, Manfred, you sound like Solly."

"Dad doesn't sound like me," Solly said. "His voice is way too low."

At six o'clock, we headed over to Kaspar Snit's house. We were surprised to see a sleek silver motor home parked in the driveway. It had curtains on the windows and inside, when we jumped up, we could see a table, a sink, and beds. "That's so cool," Solly said.

We walked up to the porch. On the door was a hand-written sign: PLEASE COME AROUND TO THE BACKYARD.

Solly asked, "You think he's going to spray us with the hose?"

I said, "Why don't you go first and find out?"

But then I changed my mind and went first instead. After all, I was the one who had insisted on believing in Kaspar Snit. So if this was a trap, it ought to be me who fell into it. As we went along the side of the house, I was surprised again, this time because I could hear music playing. And as we came to the back, what I saw made my mouth drop open.

Kaspar Snit in a tuxedo and cape.

Mrs. Leer in a wedding dress.

They were standing before Officer Yogis, under a trellis of flowers. A string quartet was playing on the lawn.

"Are you both being arrested?" Solly said.

"No," said Kaspar Snit. "Officer Yogis is also a justice of the peace."

"A piece of what?" asked Solly.

"Daisy," said Mrs. Leer, waving the bouquet of flowers in her hand. "You're just in time to be the matron of honor. If you would do me the honor."

"Oh, my goodness! Of course I would," said my mother, her hands going up to her face.

"And, *ahem*, Manfred," said Kaspar Snit. "If you could possibly see yourself as my best man. . . ."

"But I would be only too glad to," Dad said, stepping forward.

"You're getting *married*?" I said, in amazement.

"Yes, dear Eleanor," said Mrs. Leer. "I'm old-fashioned that way. And if you would be the flower girl, I would be most happy."

"Hey, don't I get to do anything?" Solly said.

"Solly, you must be the ring bearer," said Kaspar Snit.

"Shall we begin?" said Officer Yogis.

"Yes," said Kaspar Snit. "And please, no knock-knock jokes."

And so Kaspar Snit and Mrs. Leer became Lucretia and Kaspar Snit-Leer. We got to throw confetti all over them, and then Solly and I pelted each other too. When we were done, Kaspar and Lucretia – as they insisted we now call them – took us all round to the front of the house. Kaspar opened the door of the motor home.

"We're going to hit the road!" Lucretia said. "I've convinced Kaspar that we should travel. You see such wonderful places and meet such interesting people. The East Coast, the West Coast, and everything in between!"

"When are you going to come back?" Solly said.

"Who knows?" Kaspar said. "We have sold the house. I've quit my teaching job, as a service to my students. We could end up anywhere. All I'm taking is Lawrence."

"Lawrence?" said Dad.

"My pet tarantula."

"But we promise to keep in touch regularly," Lucretia said. "And you must come and visit us."

"After all," Kaspar said, "it'll always be easy for you to get a flight. See, I made a joke!"

"Keep working on it, dear," said his new wife, patting his arm. "And now we must go. We've got borders to cross before we sleep! Good-bye, darling Eleanor; good-bye, my dearest Solly! And to you, Manfred and Daisy, thank you for everything!"

The four of us waved as the motor home slowly pulled away. The horn honked three times and then the motor home was gone around the corner.

IMMORTALIZED

Our plane touched down on the runway of the Verulia International Airport. A brass band began to play and, through the window, I could see H. Waldorf Mansfield at the end of the red carpet, waiting to greet us.

"How wonderful to see you all," the ambassador said, as we came down the steps. "Eleanor, you're looking very grown-up."

"Thanks," I said. "And how is the ballet dancing going?"

"You'll have to wait until tomorrow to find out," he answered, with a wink.

From the moment that we arrived, the Verulians treated us as special guests. We were taken by limousine to our hotel in the main square. We sat at the head table for a banquet in the evening, and afterwards we watched a performance by the Verulia Amateur Dance Company, with H. Waldorf Mansfield in the leading male role. He did pretty well too – he dropped the leading female dancer only once.

The unveiling of the first fountain was held the next day at noon. Thousands of people gathered in the square, a brass band played, dignitaries made speeches from a special platform. And then a little boy, chosen from all the schoolchildren in the country, pulled the chord that lifted the giant sheet off the fountain.

"Holy superhero," said Solly. "It's *us*!"

It *was* us. Rising above a formation of clouds carved out of beautiful streaked marble were statues of Mom, Dad, Solly, and me. Flying. Mom and I were in the lead, heads forward, arms tilted back, towel capes stretched out behind us. Then came Solly, carved with goggles, bathing cap, and cape. And last was Dad, with a look on his face that seemed to say, *Hey, wait up!*

"I can't believe it," I said to my father.

He smiled at me. "It's what they wanted."

At that moment the water went on, making four graceful arcs right over the figures. The people cheered and threw flowers into the air. Fireworks exploded overhead.

Coming back home, we took a cab from the airport. I was pretty tired and kept nodding off, only to have Solly shove me off his shoulder. I blinked, shook myself, and got out of the cab.

I could hardly believe it. In front of the house was our fountain. Eight horses rearing up. Four men and four women holding conch shells spurting water. Eight naked butts.

We all stared at it. "Dad," I said, "I can't believe you got it back! How did you do it?"

"I didn't do it. Daisy?"

"Don't look at me. I thought it was gone for good."

"Look," I said, "there's a card hanging on that horse's tail."

Dad reached up and picked off the card and we all leaned together to read it.

> I wanted to complete my lessons.
> "Lesson ten: *Do something surprising.*"
> Regards, Kaspar.

"I guess he passes your course," said Mom.

"With honors," I agreed.

"But look how dirty they let it get," Dad said. "It's a disgrace. Tomorrow is definitely going to be Fountain-Cleaning Day. And no complaints!"

Mom and I smiled at each other. Dad was definitely back to his old self. We all helped carry in the luggage and, while my parents began to unpack, Solly and I went outside again. We watched the water cascading over the figures in the fountain.

"You know what?" Solly said. "First it felt weird that Kaspar Snit lived on our street and now it feels weird that he doesn't."

"Look," I said. "Somebody's moving into his house."

I could see a moving van in front of the house on the other side of the street. We watched as one of the men came out of the van with a bicycle.

"Hey, there must be a kid moving in," Solly said. "I wonder how old he is."

"Or she is," I said. "Let's go see."

We crossed the road and walked to the house. Just as we got there, the front door opened and a kid came out. It was Ginger Hirshbein.

"Ginger!" Solly said.

Ginger ran down to us. "Hi! Surprised to see me?"

"Am I ever. What are you doing here?"

"My family decided to move back. It was nice in Newfoundland, but we missed the old neighborhood. Want to come in and play? There are lots of cool boxes to make into forts."

"Sure."

"Hey, where's your Googoo-man outfit?"

"I outgrew it."

"Yeah. I outgrew my bunny pajamas."

The two of them stood there, thinking about getting older for a moment. And then they ran into the house, smacking each other on the backs of their heads as they went. I guess they weren't *that* much older.

Night. I tried to sleep, but something was bothering me. I mean, *really* bothering me. I sat up in bed, looking at the shadow objects around me – the dolls up on the shelf from when I was little, the guitar leaning in the corner, the clothes thrown over a chair. I got up and opened my door, letting it bang behind me as I made my way down the hall. It wasn't so late yet and I could see a light on under my parents' door. I went into the living room, put my hands on my hips, and in my loudest voice I shouted: "WHAT ABOUT ME!"

A moment later I heard a sound, like someone falling out of bed. My parents' bedroom door flew open and they rushed down the hall. When they got to the entrance to the living room, they stopped, their eyes wide.

"What's wrong, Eleanor?" Mom said.

"Are you sick, honey?" Dad asked.

Solly appeared behind them, rubbing the sleep from his eyes. "What's going on?" he said.

"No, I'm not sick," I said. "I'm just mad."

"Mad?" Mom said.

"Yes, mad. When is it going to be my turn to have a problem? I mean, first Dad lost his job. Then Mom couldn't fly. Then Solly didn't want to be Googoo-man anymore. And then Kaspar Snit wanted to be good. When is it my turn, huh? When do I get to be the one everybody is worried about?"

They all looked at me. "You're friggin' nuts," Solly said.

"No, Eleanor isn't nuts," said Mom. "It's true. We've all been so concerned for ourselves that we haven't been paying any attention to her."

"That's absolutely correct," said Dad. "Eleanor, we apologize. From the bottom of our hearts. So please give us a chance. We're listening. We *want* to know what is bothering you . . . what your problem is. Tell us."

I looked at each of them as they waited for me to speak. Finally I looked down. "I can't think of anything right now."

"Well, when you do think of something, let us know," Mom said.

"Absolutely," Dad agreed. "You let us know."

"I was right," Solly said. "You *are* friggin' nuts."

Embarrassed, I turned to the window. But it was true, I couldn't think of anything that was wrong. I said, "Could we go for a fly? I mean, all of us, as a family. It's been a long time."

"What a lovely idea," Dad said. "But I'm not sure that Mom is, you know, up to it."

"I'd like to try," Mom said. "I might be ready. But I need a refill." She held out her hand. "I'm all out."

"Me too," said Dad.

"Me three," said Solly.

They all lined up – Mom, Dad, and Solly – and I pressed my palm to each of theirs in turn. Every time, the image of a quarter moon and three stars became imprinted on theirs. Then I went to the window, glanced back at the others, and got into position. A moment later, I could feel the night air on my face.

When I opened my eyes, I saw the branches of a tree near me, the wide leaves shimmering gently. Then Solly came up beside me just before flying ahead. Dad followed, crying *ouch!* as he scraped the top of his head on the branches. "I better follow that brother of yours before he gets too far," Dad said, heading out.

I waited, hovering there. I waited longer. Then suddenly I heard a soft sound and turned to see Mom hovering next to me.

"Hey, I'm up!" she said, smiling.

"How does it feel?" I asked.

"It feels *gooood*. You coming?"

"In a sec, Mom."

"Okay. Don't get too far behind."

Mom altered one shoulder – she was an elegant flyer – and banked away. I wanted to stay by myself a moment, feeling the night all around me. I heard a rustling sound and, looking closely, saw a bird perched on a branch of the tree.

It was a pigeon. It had something in its beak. Something shiny.

It draped the shiny thing onto the branch and then cooed before fluttering higher up into the tree.

I reached out carefully, so as not to lose my balance, and picked up the shiny thing. It was a silver chain with something dangling on it. I brought it closer to my face so that I could see it in the dark, but just by feeling it, I already knew.

The amulet.

Had the pigeon brought it back on purpose? I didn't think that was possible, but here it was in my hand. I put it around my neck for safekeeping – after all, it belonged in the museum in Verulia, and now we could give it back.

Suddenly I felt so light and happy – I didn't have any words for it. I rose higher, over the tree, and seeing the flying shapes of my family up ahead, I put on some speed and glided through the night to catch up.